REVERSAL OF FORTUNE

A CLAIRE ROLLINS MYSTERY BOOK 2

J. A. WHITING

J. A. WHITING BOOKS

To hear about new books and book sales, please sign up for my mailing list at:
www.jawhiting.com

 Created with Vellum

For my family with love

Claire Rollins and her best friend, Nicole, sat on the red velvet seats in the balcony of City Opera House listening to a chorus singing the words to a classic show tune while members of the resident ballet company performed on the stage. Their co-worker, Robby, a twenty-one-year-old music student, had completed a solo and his voice was so magically beautiful that Claire almost jumped to her feet to applaud before catching herself. She and Nicole exchanged wide-eyed looks, both marveling at Robby's amazing talent. Before Robby started his solo, Claire's body filled with nervousness for her young friend, hoping for him to do his best.

Claire glanced around the opera house

entranced by the beauty of the building, the red drapes hanging elegantly over the sides of the stage, the cream and gold painted walls, the intricate carvings and moldings, the lighting, the cut glass chandeliers, and the painted scene on the center of the ceiling, all nearly made her jaw drop. Feeling like a queen in a castle, she leaned back comfortably against her seat to enjoy the rest of the musical event.

In the lobby amongst a throng of theatre-goers leaving the building after the performance, Claire and Nicole moved toward the front doors. "That was amazing." Claire felt exhilarated by the musical event.

"Robby was unbelievable," Nicole added. "I think I'm going to encourage him to be a singing waiter at the chocolate shop. I'll even pay him extra."

When Claire chuckled, her long, soft, blond curls bounced over her shoulders. "Good idea. You'll double your business for sure if Robby sings while he prepares the customers' drinks and serves the sweets."

"Nicole!" Someone called.

Nicole turned around to see her friend, Vanessa Dodd, hurrying over. The girls hugged.

"Wasn't that terrific?" Vanessa smiled. "I haven't seen you in months and I run into you here."

Nicole introduced Claire, and Vanessa introduced her younger sister, Maddy. "Maddy will be a sophomore at MIT this fall. Since I work in Kendall Square, we decided we're going to find an apartment together."

Nicole and Vanessa grew up in Greendale, a small town about twenty minutes west of Boston. In high school, the two had played sports together and occasionally hung out in a group of friends, but drifted apart when they went off to college. With Vanessa back in the city, she and Nicole had reconnected and met for dinner or a drink about once a month.

"How's your business doing?" Vanessa was tall and athletic and her long brown hair tumbled halfway down her back. Maddy seemed a miniature version of her sister, almost a full four inches shorter than Vanessa, but with the same wide smile and long dark hair.

"It's doing really well. We're so busy most mornings, I'm probably going to have to hire more help."

"One of our co-workers performed tonight," Claire said.

"Really? Who was it?" Vanessa asked. "I don't

know anyone with talent like the people on that stage."

Claire explained who Robby was and what he had sung during his solo.

Maddy's eyes widened. "You know him? His voice is incredible." Her lips formed into a pretty smile. "Is he single?"

"Yeah, he's single," Nicole said and raised an eyebrow. "But he's batting for the other team, if you know what I mean."

Maddy's face took on an expression of puzzlement and then Nicole's meaning dawned on her and she sadly shook her head. "Why are all the good ones gay?"

"There must be tons of great guys at MIT," Claire said.

Maddy moaned. "They're all so busy with their work that they don't have time for anything else."

After a few minutes more of conversation, Vanessa said, "We need to get going. Maddy has to catch the train back to Greendale and I'm taking the train to New York City tonight for a business meeting in the morning." The foursome said their goodbyes with promises to get together soon. Claire shook hands with both of the young women and told them how nice it was to meet them. Outside in the warm summer night air, Nicole and Claire strolled along the busy city sidewalks as tourists and residents headed to restaurants and bars, live shows, or to evening museum events.

"Too bad we have to be up early tomorrow morning." Nicole swung the long strap of her clutch over her shoulder. "It would be fun to go out for a glass of wine somewhere."

"We can stop for a drink." Claire watched the people hurrying along. Some were dressed in evening clothes, long dresses, well-tailored suits, and others wore jeans and suit jackets or casual summer dresses. Professionals, college students, happy tourists moved together across the city. Claire loved the historic place with its old buildings, brick sidewalks, beautiful parks, brownstones, universities, shopping, waterfront, and modern buildings, all perfectly working together to create a vibrant, walkable, livable town.

"Okay, let's have one and then we can head home." Nicole spotted two stools being vacated at an outside bar and swooped in to take them.

"Good eyes," Claire complimented her friend. "And very speedy. Maybe *you* should be training for the mini-triathlon."

"Not me." Nicole shook her head vigorously.

"Never in a million years. I'll leave that foolishness to you and your handsome detective friend."

Claire's cheeks turned pink at the reference to Ian Fuller, the detective that she and Nicole had met a few weeks ago when they were dragged into a murder case. Ian and Claire had been training together to compete in an upcoming triathlon.

The bartender delivered the glasses of wine and Claire and Nicole sipped. It was a perfect summer evening with the air still warm and a pleasant gentle breeze off the ocean. The buzz of conversations around them was occasionally punctuated with a high-spirited laugh as people enjoyed mingling, flirting, and chatting.

"Tell me about your hometown," Claire suggested.

"It was a nice place to grow up." Nicole set her glass down. "So close to the city, but it still had the feeling of a small town. Nice parks and green space, tall trees, pretty neighborhoods. Big, beautiful old houses. The main street is fun, there are shops and restaurants and boutiques, and the library. I'll take you there someday for lunch and we can walk around."

"I'd love that."

"I don't know many people there now. My friends

all moved away. My parents are gone, my sister is in D.C." Nicole pushed a stray strand of dark brown hair from her eyes. "Vanessa's parents still live there so that's one family left from when I used to live in the town. Maddy's living at home with them until school starts at the end of August."

"What does Vanessa do for work?" Claire asked.

"She's an accountant. She works for a CPA firm. To me, that sounds boring, but to each his own." Nicole smiled. "I much prefer to be on my feet all day, buzzing around the chocolate shop."

"I couldn't see you sitting at a desk for hours. Nuh-uh. That definitely wouldn't work." Claire chuckled. "Do you know what the sister is studying?"

"Electrical engineering." Nicole shook her head. "Another subject not for me. Vanessa told me that Maddy has always loved math and science, she's a natural."

Back at the Opera House, Claire had sensed something sad about Maddy. "Has Maddy had to deal with something serious lately?"

Nicole made eye contact with her friend. "Serious? How do you mean?"

Claire blinked and gave a slight shake of her head. "I don't know. I just wondered."

With wide eyes, Nicole stared at Claire. "You don't know? You ask me if Maddy has had some problem lately and then you say you don't know? What's going on Claire?"

A feeling of anxiety mixed with unease flitted over Claire's skin and made her shiver. "I just ... wondered."

"You said that already." Nicole's eyes bored into Claire's. "That's an odd thing to wonder about without any cause. Maddy didn't hint at such a thing and neither did Vanessa. So...."

"So what?" Claire was sorry she'd brought it up. She lifted her wine glass and took a swallow. Ever since her husband died and she'd moved to Boston just over a year ago, thirty-five-year-old Claire had developed the uncanny capability of being able to sometimes *sense* things from people. She called it strong intuition. Nicole called it paranormal ability.

"Oh, no." Nicole leaned closer. "You got a *feeling*, didn't you?"

"No. Well ... I might have." Claire looked out over the crowd of people standing at the bar and sitting at the outside tables.

"What did you feel?" Nicole wasn't going to let her friend weasel out of it. "Claire. Tell me. We aren't going anywhere until you tell me what's going on."

Claire swallowed. "Oh, okay. Just for the record, you should give up the chocolate shop and become an investigator. You'd wear down the witness and get a confession every time." Shaking her head, Claire went on. "When I shook Maddy's hand, I felt something."

"I knew it." Worry washed over Nicole's face. "She's not in danger is she? Should we warn her?"

Claire cocked her head. "Really? What would you say? Claire had a feeling? She'd think you were crazy. Anyway, no, I didn't get the sense that Maddy was in danger. It was more ... sadness, anger, grief ... an injustice? I don't know. She might have broken up with a boyfriend? Maybe she had a disagreement with someone? It's probably nothing."

"What kind of a disagreement?"

Claire stared at Nicole. "I have no idea. I just got a quick sensation. It's most likely groundless." Although she wanted nothing more than to brush the whole thing off, Claire had a growing sense of dread filling her chest. "I think we should go home. It's getting late."

Nicole grinned. "Trying to deflect having any more conversation on the subject?"

They slipped from the stools and headed off down the sidewalk. As they were about to part ways for their own apartments, Nicole's phone rang. Claire watched her friend's face pale under the streetlamp. "I will. Okay. I'll take care of it."

Nicole ended the call, grabbed Claire's arm, and stuck her hand out to hail a passing cab. "You have to come with me." Nicole's voice shook. "That was Vanessa. She's on the train to New York. Maddy just called her, hysterical. She said something about the police, about their mom. Vanessa asked me to go to the house to see what's going on."

Nicole swung open the cab door. Before getting in, she looked at Claire for a moment. "You were right. Your feeling was right. Again."

2

As the cab moved through the quiet streets of Greendale, Claire could see large expensive homes sitting on well-tended, lushly landscaped lots set back from the road. A flash of blue lights up ahead caused Claire to lean forward so she could see through the front windshield. Feelings of dread slipped down her throat. Police cars and an ambulance were parked in front of a three-story wood shingled home with a black wrought-iron fence running around the front property line. Every light in the house blazed through the windows and people moved like shadows in one of the upper rooms.

An officer flagged the cab to stop and Claire and Nicole jumped out.

The officer raised a hand in a *halt* gesture. "No one's allowed near the house."

Nicole stepped up to the man. "Our friend called minutes ago. This is her parents' home. She asked us to come. She's afraid for her sister."

The officer seemed to be deciding what to do with the information.

"The friend is Vanessa Dodd. She told me her sister is here and is completely distraught. Maddy Dodd, she's nineteen. Vanessa asked us to come and see about her sister."

The officer hesitated and was about to speak, when Claire pointed at the walkie-talkie attached to the man's chest. "Maybe you could talk to your supervisor or the person in charge. Ask permission for us to talk to Maddy."

A woman's mournful wail pierced the night air sending shivers down Claire's back. Nicole stepped to the side of the man to get a look at what was happening in front of the house.

Attendants hurriedly pushed a gurney towards the waiting ambulance that had its doors flung open allowing yellow light to flood over the sidewalk. A white sheet covered the form on the stretcher up to the person's chin. Nicole squinted trying to see who the victim was. "Is it Mrs. Dodd?" She turned to the officer with a horrified expression. "What happened here? Where's Maddy?"

Claire moved a few yards to the right to get a better vantage point. Police officers and an official-looking man and woman moved about the front and side yards. A woman clutched the arm of a petite brunette as they crossed the front lawn of the property.

"There she is." Claire pointed.

Nicole called out to Maddy and the young woman blinked in their direction until she recognized the person waving at her. "Nicole!" Maddy took several steps toward Nicole and Claire, but stumbled and fell to her knees.

Nicole and Claire ran to the side of the sobbing nineteen-year-old. "What's happened Maddy?" Nicole knelt and put her arms around the young woman.

Claire looked at the sixty-something woman, a petite blond, wearing a gray sweater and sweat pants, who had been trying to help Maddy. "What happened?"

"I'm a neighbor." A look of shock played over the woman's face, her eyes wide. "I'm a family friend.

Lorraine Hale. I was awake reading in the den. Maddy was in the yard screaming. The police car pulled up as I was running over here."

Claire held the woman's eyes. "What happened?" she asked more firmly.

"Grace." Lorraine pointed to the ambulance as it pulled away. "She ... she fell." The woman waved her hand toward the side of the house. "From the third floor."

Shifting her gaze to the upper floor of the home, Claire could see that most of the activity going on inside was in the room Lorraine had pointed to. The window was wide open and someone was taking photographs in the room.

Maddy sat on the sidewalk, her head in her hands. "Mom. Mom. Dad said she fell. Mom was on the ground." A choking sound escaped the young woman's throat.

"Is she...?" Claire asked.

Lorraine brushed at her eyes. "Grace is still alive. She was still breathing."

"You got here before the ambulance arrived?" Claire glanced around at the activity in the front yard.

Lorraine nodded. "I crossed the street. I ran to Maddy. She was kneeling beside her mother."

"Did Grace speak?"

"She was unconscious, but I could see her chest rising and falling." Lorraine wrung her hands together.

"Your mother fell from the window?" Claire knelt beside Maddy.

Maddy nodded.

"What happened when you got here?" Claire asked in a gentle voice. "You took the train home?"

Maddy swallowed. "I headed for the front porch. I saw the front door was open. I got worried. I called for my parents. No one answered." Maddy's breathing was ragged and rapid. "I found Dad in his office. He was holding Mom's raincoat. He seemed really nervous. I asked him what was going on."

"What did he say?" Nicole put her arm around Maddy's shoulders.

"He didn't say anything. He just stood there with a weird look on his face." The young woman's voice cracked, and then she clutched her arms around her knees and began to rock back and forth.

A woman police officer came and spoke calmly to Maddy, helped her up, and led her to the house, Claire assumed for questioning. She was amazed that the police had left Maddy alone for so long and she'd been able to ask the girl a few questions.

"Maddy was with her mother when you got here?" Claire asked.

Lorraine nodded. "I could see Grace was breathing. She was wearing a nightgown. There was blood all over her. She had cuts everywhere. Maddy was holding her hand, telling her everything would be okay." The woman's voice hitched.

"Where was Mr. Dodd? Was he outside?"

"Ronald came out and put a raincoat over Grace. Then he walked away and I didn't see him again."

"Did he tell you what happened?"

"Ronald said Grace fell out of the window. I asked why she was upstairs. Ronald said he didn't know, that he was on the first floor when it happened. He walked away. I didn't pay attention to where he went. Why was she up there? Grace hardly ever went up to the third floor." The woman burst into tears.

Claire wrapped her arms around the woman until a man, his hair mussed and wearing pajamas and a bathrobe, hurried across the street to his wife.

Nicole took Claire's arm and moved her down the street away from the hubbub. "I have to call Vanessa. What on earth am I going to tell her?"

"Tell her what you know, but start with the fact that her mother is still alive."

While Nicole made the dreaded call, Claire watched the goings-on around the huge house.

Clicking off from the phone conversation, Nicole said, "Vanessa is on her way here. She got off the train at the first stop it made and hopped the next train returning to Boston. She'll grab a cab to the hospital. She won't be back for another two hours. She's been trying to reach her father, but he doesn't pick up."

"He's probably still talking to the police," Claire said. "Do you want to meet Vanessa at the hospital?"

"She said to head home. She'll call tomorrow with updates."

Claire kept her eyes on the authorities who were buzzing around the crime scene. Anxiety made her feel slightly sick. "What are these people like?"

Nicole faced her friend. "What do you mean?"

"Obviously from the look of the house and the property and the neighborhood, they're a wealthy family. What are they like? How do they get along?"

"They always seemed nice. The mom was always kind, friendly, good to the girls, nice to me." Nicole placed her hand on the side of her face. "The dad is a doctor, a cardiologist. Grace is a professor, she teaches in the city. I don't think either one has retired yet, but I'm not sure."

"What does she teach?"

"Public policy."

"Did the parents get along?" Claire asked.

"Yeah. It seemed so. They used to do a lot together, golf, go to dinner, entertain. They were active in the community. I haven't seen them for years though." Nicole wrapped her arms around herself. "I can't believe this happened."

"How about Vanessa and Maddy ... did they get along with the parents?"

"Vanessa definitely did. Maddy was just a little kid when I was in high school. I don't think Dr. Dodd was around much, he was always working, but Vanessa talked fondly of him. She was super close to her mom. They did things together all the time. Vanessa genuinely liked being around her. I'd assume Maddy felt the same way."

Claire made eye contact with her friend. "What's the layout of the house?"

Nicole faced the building trying to remember. "There's a foyer when you step in. There's a dining room and living room to the left and an office to the right. There's a big kitchen and family room off the back, they added those spaces to the house when I was in high school. Oh, there's a small sunroom off the kitchen."

"How about the upper floors?"

"Bedrooms and baths on the second floor. I don't remember how many. There's a staircase to the third floor."

"What's up there?"

"Two guest bedrooms, a bath, and a big room sort of like another family room. We never spent any time up there. We used the family room on the first floor."

"Does their mother have an office in the house?" Claire asked.

"Yeah, she did. She used one of the bedrooms on the second floor for that. I don't recall anyone spending time on the third floor. Vanessa said they all joked how they should remove that floor from the house, then they wouldn't have to heat it or cool it."

"Was Grace ever depressed?"

Worry caused Nicole's voice to tremble. "You don't think it was an accident? You think she might have deliberately jumped?"

"I have no idea." Claire gave a shrug. "Was she ever depressed when you knew her?"

"Never, but I didn't see a lot of her." Nicole's jaw muscles tensed. "She was always happy, positive, upbeat whenever I was around."

"Well, maybe she hid it well," Claire said.

"Maybe something finally caught up with her and she couldn't take it anymore."

Even as Claire said those words, she had to admit she didn't believe them. Not one bit.

3

Claire, sitting in Tony's Deli and Market with her two rescue Corgis, Lady and Bear, resting on the floor next to her table, gave Tony and Augustus Gunther a run-down on how she'd spent the hours after watching the show at the Opera House the previous night.

Augustus, a former lawyer and judge in his early nineties, listened carefully while sipping from his mug of tea. He adjusted his bow tie and leaned forward. "Do you get the impression that the woman jumped or fell from the window?"

"I honestly have no idea." Claire reached down and patted Bear's soft fur.

Tony said, "When the woman regains consciousness, she'll be able to explain what happened." In his early seventies, Tony had owned the deli and small market for over fifty years.

"It would be interesting to hear what the husband has to say," Augustus said. "He told the neighbor that Mrs. Dodd *fell* from the window, correct?"

"That's what she told me." Claire stood and went to the small coffee and tea bar set up in a tiny corner of the deli to refill her teacup.

"No one else was home at the time?" Augustus questioned.

"The younger daughter arrived home shortly after the accident happened." Claire paid Tony for a blueberry muffin.

"How did that woman fall out of a window?" Tony grumped. "Was it closed? Did it have a screen on it? How the heck did it happen? How often do you hear of people falling out of windows? Was she drunk?"

"I don't know," Claire said again. "I don't know the people. I just met the two daughters last night."

"But Nicole knows the family," Tony said. "She must know if the woman has a substance-abuse problem."

"That could have happened after Nicole left town to go to college." Claire gave a shrug. "Nicole hasn't lived in Greendale for over ten years. A lot can change in ten years."

"Hopefully, the woman will fully recover and won't have any lasting injuries." Tony picked up his broom and swept the crumbs from the floor near the tea-coffee bar. "Imagine falling out of a three-story building." The stocky man gave a shudder. "I'd have a heart attack on the way down."

Claire imagined the horror of falling from a high place knowing you were about to hit the ground and waiting those long seconds for the impact. Her mind ran over the possibilities that could have led to the fall. The night was warm and pleasant. Was the window open already? Did Mrs. Dodd trip, lose her balance, and go out the window? Was she opening or closing the window and got dizzy? Was there any other way the woman went out? Claire's heart skipped a beat. She may have jumped or someone....

Shaking herself back to the conversation, Claire heard Augustus say, "Perhaps Mrs. Dodd's husband had a hand in the accident."

"Dr. Dodd told the neighbor he was on the first floor when his wife fell."

One of Augustus's bushy eyebrows rose up. "So the man says."

Shivers of worry ran up and down Claire's back.

"Was anyone else in the house to corroborate the man's claim?" Augustus eyed Claire.

"I think they were the only ones at home when it happened."

"Hmm," was all Augustus said in response.

Bear and Lady both whined in unison at the moment Claire's phone buzzed with a text from Nicole. Her fingers trembled slightly when she reached for the phone and a gasp of breath slipped from her throat when she read the words on the small screen. "Mrs. Dodd has passed away from her injuries." Claire lifted her eyes to Augustus and then Tony. "She never regained consciousness."

"A terrible shame." Tony shook his head sadly. "A split second thing can change everything."

The three pondered the news in silence for a minute and then Claire picked up her mug and headed to place it in the plastic bin of dirty dishes on top of the trash can. "I'd better get to work." She bent to pat the dogs. "Be good while I'm at work." Bear and Lady often spent the day at Tony's deli while Claire went to her job at Nicole's chocolate shop in Boston's North End. "Thanks for dog-sitting." She gave Tony a hug. "See you later this afternoon."

Claire nodded at Augustus. "Talk to you later."

"Indeed." Augustus lifted his mug to the young woman.

They both knew that there would be plenty to talk about very soon and that it would involve what had happened to Mrs. Grace Dodd.

WHEN CLAIRE OPENED the door to the chocolate shop, her eyes went wide. Vanessa Dodd sat at a table with Nicole, a crumpled tissue held tight in her hand. Nicole waved Claire over.

Vanessa looked up. "Claire. Sit with us."

Claire mumbled her condolences.

Nicole turned her eyes to her friend. "Vanessa wants us to help with something."

The words sent a chill over Claire's skin.

"Vanessa knows we were involved in the airport case last month." Claire and Nicole had been out walking in the city one night and were on the sidewalk when a person in a car drove past and fired shots into the crowd. One thing led to another until the friends were knee-deep in the mystery.

Vanessa explained. "The police are going to rule that my mother committed suicide." She had to stop speaking for a few moments and then her face hardened. "My mother *did not* kill herself."

"She wants us to look into the accident." Nicole's facial expression was serious.

Claire's breath caught in her chest. The last thing she wanted was to get mixed up in the mess. "But--"

Vanessa cut her off. "I know what you're going to say. You're going to say you don't have the training or experience necessary to investigate. You're going to tell me that you aren't law enforcement officers or detectives. You're going to tell me to go talk to the police."

Claire thought Vanessa had pretty much nailed it.

"Next you'll tell me to hire a private investigator."

Claire hadn't thought of that. "A private investigator is probably a good idea."

Vanessa shook her head. "I want someone I know and trust. You and Nicole discovered a lot of information on that airport case. People are more likely to talk to regular individuals ... they'll open up more than when they talk to the police. People get intimidated by the police. If a woman talks to them about something that's happened, they're more trusting, they'll give more information."

"She's right," Nicole said.

Claire held her friend's eyes and Nicole could tell that Claire didn't want anything to do with the problem so she made a suggestion. "We could start with a few people and see how it goes."

Vanessa's face flooded with such hope that it made Claire's heart contract. "If you want us to talk to people, I guess we could try. But first, we'll need to talk to you. I'll have to ask some hard questions, nosy questions. I'm going to have to ask things about your family's private lives and if you aren't up-front about it, we may as well give up now."

"I'll answer truthfully." Vanessa looked straight into Claire's eyes. "I promise."

"I need to ask you," Claire said, "what help will it be if we talk to people about this, even if something comes from our discussions? Anything we find out will be called hearsay. The police won't take it seriously."

Vanessa's jaw set. "I have to know."

Nicole leaned forward from the other side of the table. "Her father is saying things that don't add up. His story is different every time."

"Could that be from shock?" Claire questioned.

"It seems like more than shock." Vanessa cleared her throat. "It seems ... deceptive."

"Why do you think so?"

"When I arrived at the hospital last night, my father wasn't there. Maddy was there holding Mom's hand. I asked her where Dad was. She said he was still talking to the police." Vanessa's face clouded. "How could he have been talking to the police all that time? Why didn't he come to the hospital?"

Claire asked, "Couldn't he have been with the police?"

"There's more," Nicole answered.

"Mom passed away a few hours after I got to the hospital. Maddy and I went home together. The hospital had called Dad to let him know. When we got home, Dad was sitting in an easy chair in his office looking off into space. I tried to talk to him. He was acting like a zombie. At first, I thought his behavior *was* due to shock, but when I asked him questions, he was evasive. I asked him what happened. He told me he didn't know. He said he'd been resting on his bed because he'd had a headache. He'd taken a sleeping pill." Vanessa blew out a breath. "Earlier, he'd told our neighbor that he was on the *first* floor when the accident happened. His bedroom is on the second floor. Which was it? How could he be that confused? He doesn't even remember where he was when Mom fell?"

Claire was about to say something when Nicole

repeated what she'd said a minute ago. "There's more."

Claire looked at Vanessa waiting for her to add to what she'd been telling.

"Dad told me not to talk to the police. He told me if anyone seemed like they were about to present me with a summons then I should pretend I was someone else. He said, 'Be sure Maddy does the same.'" Vanessa shook her head. "Why would he ask me to do that? Because he's trying to hide something? Will you talk to some people? Find out what they know? Please?" The pitch of Vanessa's voice rose higher. "I don't know what's going on. Did my father do this? Did he push my mother from the window? Why is he acting so strangely?"

Nicole and Claire exchanged glances.

"Well, I guess we could talk to Maddy and the neighbor we saw at the house last night," Nicole said. "Then we can decide if it's worth talking to anyone else. Is that okay?"

"That's a good way to start." A grateful smile spread over Vanessa's face.

A few customers entered the chocolate shop and Nicole stood to wait on them. "We'll talk later today. I'll call you."

"I'd better get to work, too." Claire was about to

get up from her chair, but paused and put her hand on Vanessa's shoulder. "We'll do what we can to help." Little zips of electricity seemed to nip at Claire's hand where it came into contact with Vanessa's shoulder and a wave of unease engulfed her as a question came into her mind. "Can I ask you something? How was your parents' relationship? Were they getting along?"

Vanessa stiffened. "They were cordial."

Vanessa's description surprised Claire. "Only cordial?"

Taking her leather bag from the chair next to her, Vanessa stood to go. "Dad was having an affair."

4

Nicole and Claire entered the living room of Vanessa's Cambridge apartment. The small space had high ceilings which made the room seem much bigger and the large windows gave a good view of the evening bustle on Massachusetts Avenue. A collection of framed family photographs stood on the side table behind the sofa and Claire bent to look at the ones with Dr. Dodd in them.

Nicole had brought a box of assorted cookies from the chocolate shop and placed it in the center of the coffee table.

"I found out about two months ago that my father was having an affair. It had been going on for about six months. Mom was suspicious and she confronted Dad. He admitted it right away. I arrived for dinner right after they'd had a blowout over it." Vanessa let out a sigh. "Needless to say, we didn't sit down to dinner and nice conversation that evening."

"What happened when you arrived?" Nicole asked. She couldn't imagine walking into a mess like that. "What did you do?"

"Mom was hysterical. I've never seen her like that before. Ever. She had marks on her arm. She said Dad had grabbed her. She was crying. Dad had a scratch on his face, I assumed from my mother pushing at him to let her go." Vanessa closed her eyes for several moments and when she spoke, her voice was just above a whisper. "It was so awful."

"How was your father?" Claire asked.

"He was subdued." Vanessa shook her head. "He seemed almost detached from my mother's upset. When Mom left the room for a while, Dad answered some of my questions. He said he'd met the woman while golfing. He said she was nice to talk to, she had lots of interests, she knew politics and current events. It was like he needed to defend his transgression, like he had to inform me about how intelligent this woman was. I was appalled. He told me that she was a good person, had come from a good family. Didn't he think his stupid babbling over the woman would bother me? He was cheating on *my mother*, for God's sake."

"Did you stay at the house?" Nicole looked upset over what she'd heard.

"I talked to my mom for a while. I couldn't stand speaking to my father for another minute. I didn't even want to be in the same room with him. Mom and I went up to her office on the second floor. She talked for a long time about how she felt betrayed. They'd been married for forty-five years. She talked about divorce at first, but by the end of our conversation, she thought she would wait before deciding to leave Dad. She needed time to process the whole thing."

Claire asked, "Your father halted the relationship with the other woman?"

"I don't know. He claimed he would. Mom thinks he ended it." Vanessa blinked. "*Thought* ... past tense. She thought he ended the relationship." The heartbroken young woman leaned forward and hung her head with her dark hair nearly covering her face. "I can't help but think that my father is responsible for my mother's death."

Nicole's hand went to her throat. "You think...."

Vanessa didn't look up. "I don't know if it was by

his hand or not, but his foolish affair is the reason my mother is dead. I just know it."

Claire asked gently, "What was your mother's mental state? Could she have taken her own life?"

Vanessa's head shot up, her eyes flashing. "Absolutely not. My mother would never have jumped from that window."

Claire knew that people did things they wouldn't normally do when under duress. "Did your parents drink? Do either of them take medication?"

"What does that mean?" Vanessa challenged.

"I mean," Claire said slowly, "maybe your mother and father had a few drinks that night. Maybe she and your father had words about the affair. Maybe she was so distraught that--"

Vanessa held up her hand in a "stop" gesture. "No. No matter how upset my mother might have been, she would never do anything that would take her away from Maddy and me. No. She did not jump from that window."

"Have any reports come back from the medical examiner?" Nicole asked. "That information could shed some light on what might have happened."

"Nothing is back yet. Tomorrow, possibly." Vanessa's anger over the suggestion that her mother might have taken her life seemed to fade and her energy seemed to flag as she leaned against the sofa, her shoulders sagging.

"You said that you'd like us to talk to some people." Claire moved the discussion in a different direction. "Who should we start with?"

Vanessa adjusted her position on the sofa and sat up straighter trying to collect herself. "I'd like you to talk to the neighbor. Lorraine Hale. She and her husband were friends of my parents. Lorraine was a close friend of my mother's for years. She might tell you things she wouldn't say to me."

"Is there someone else you'd like us to speak with?" Nicole asked.

"My father." Vanessa's words were hard. "I want you to talk to him. I'll show you the room, the window where Mom fell from."

When she heard that Vanessa wanted them to talk to her father, Claire's stomach lurched. The man must be in a terrible state and talking to him would seem intrusive. Trying to think of reasons she could voice against paying the man a visit, Vanessa headed off her concerns.

"I know Dad is in a delicate state right now, but I think this is the time to question him. He might let something slip. He might not be able to keep his guard up."

Nicole looked as wary as Claire did. "When do you want us to visit him?"

"Tomorrow night. As soon as we finish talking here, I'm going to Dad's house. I'm going to move back there for a while." Vanessa's eyes darkened. "Maddy's living in the house. I don't want her home alone with Dad. Can you make it tomorrow night?"

Nicole took a quick look at Claire and then said, "I guess we could come over tomorrow."

Vanessa suggested a time and the girls agreed.

"What else can you tell us?" Claire asked. "Do you know the name of the woman your father was seeing?" Claire noticed Vanessa's jaw tighten as she took in a long breath.

"I know her name." Vanessa didn't say anything for half a minute. "Her name is Victoria Lowe."

The name sounded familiar to Claire, but she couldn't immediately place it.

Nicole spoke up. "Victoria Lowe? She's a state representative, isn't she?"

Vanessa gave a slight nod.

"Wow. Victoria Lowe's husband is a political advisor. He works in D.C. Obviously, no one knows about the affair. It would be all over the news."

Tension squeezed Claire's stomach. "Do you know Victoria Lowe?"

"I met her once," Vanessa said. "Dad took all of us to a political fundraiser in Boston. It was a big deal with lots of important people. He introduced us to Representative Lowe ... me, Maddy, *and* mom." Vanessa smiled, but it looked like more of a grimace. "Dad was in the middle of an affair with the woman and he had the gall to introduce us to her. Can you imagine? I feel like I don't even know him anymore. He makes me sick."

"Should we talk to Victoria Lowe?" Nicole asked. "See if your father is still seeing her?"

"I don't think there's any use. She'd never admit to it," Claire said. "Especially now, under the circumstances. She wouldn't want to get pulled into the whole mess. I imagine that Ms. Lowe wouldn't want to get between Dr. Dodd and the family. I'm sure she would want to protect him."

"That's true." Nicole deflated.

"Is there anything else you can remember about talking to your father the morning after the accident?" Claire asked.

Vanessa thought back on her interaction with her father. "Just his odd request not to talk to the authorities, not to let Maddy talk to them. And he seemed so disconnected, so spaced out."

"How is Maddy doing?" Nicole asked.

"She's a mess." Tears gathered in Vanessa's eyes. "She's been sleeping most of the time. That's one of the reasons I need to move back into the house for a while." Wiping her eyes with the back of her hand, she added, "The other reason is to find out what happened to my mother." Vanessa took a quick look at her phone to check the time. "I should get going. I want to get to the house." She stood up and thanked Nicole and Claire for their help, and taking Nicole's hand, she said, "I've known you for a long time. There aren't many people I'd trust to ask for help in this thing. Thank you for being here for me."

Nicole and Vanessa hugged.

"I need to run. I worry about Maddy being in the house with Dad. I don't trust him. I'll walk out with you."

Vanessa grabbed a small rolling suitcase and locked the apartment door before descending the staircase to the first floor of the building with Nicole and Claire. Outside on the sidewalk, Vanessa dropped her wallet when fumbling for a credit card for the cab. Claire picked it up and handed it back, and when she did, she brushed hands with the young woman causing a ping in Claire's brain.

The cab pulled to the curb, but before Vanessa

got in, Claire asked, "Did Maddy say anything about how your father looked last night?"

Vanessa turned and thought back to the previous evening when she was sitting with her sister at the hospital and her eyebrows raised. "Maddy said Dad looked spaced out. She said he had blood on the side of his face." Vanessa breathed deeply. "When I talked to him at the house, Dad had scratch marks on his temple and on his cheek. Why the heck would he have fresh scratches on his face?"

A look of anger flashed over Vanessa's face as she turned around to get into the cab.

Claire and Nicole stared at each other.

"Why *would* Dr. Dodd have blood and scratches on his face?" Claire asked. "There must be other reasons besides having an argument with his wife."

Nicole started for the subway station. "Maybe, but it doesn't sound good, does it?"

5

Running down Beacon Street past the State House with her training partner, Detective Ian Fuller, Claire suddenly sprinted off toward the Boston Common. Ian caught up to her just as she reached the grassy hill where her dogs were playing.

"Why have I not caught on yet that you always try to beat me back here?" Ian used the end of his t-shirt to wipe some sweat from his brow.

Claire chuckled. "I could never beat you unless I take off when you least expect it." She pointed to her head. "Brains over brawn."

"We're training *with* each other. We aren't racing each other."

"I know." Claire grinned, pushing an unruly

strand of her curly blond hair over her ear. "But it's fun to beat you."

Bear and Lady spotted the return of the two athletes and they took off like rockets down the green hill to welcome Claire and Ian back to the Common. So that she and Ian could go on the training run, Claire had left her Corgis with a friend who often brought her Westie to the grassy hill to play with the other dogs. When the friend had an errand to do or wanted to exercise, she left her little white dog with Claire and the Corgis.

Lady and Bear danced around the two people and then dashed off, turned speedily, and raced back to the couple. They repeated the action two more times until Claire and Ian roared with laughter at the canines' nutty antics.

"Where do those two get all their energy?" Ian bought two cold bottles of water from a vendor and handed one to Claire.

"I wish I knew. I'd like to capture some of it for myself." Claire opened her bottle and guzzled. Sweat caused her long bangs to stick to her forehead.

The two tired runners found a shady spot under a large Maple tree and sat down to watch Lady and Bear run and jump and chase the other dogs.

"How's your friend doing?" Ian asked.

"She's Nicole's friend. They've known each other for years. I only met Vanessa the other night." Claire poured some water into her hand and splashed it onto her face. "She's not doing great. Vanessa is suspicious of her father. She claims her mother would never have committed suicide." Spending the next fifteen minutes telling Ian what she'd learned from Vanessa about what happened the other night, but leaving out who Dr. Dodd was having an affair with, Claire paused, pulled her legs up, and wrapped her arms around her knees. "It could have been an accident, but I'm worried that the doctor pushed his wife. His behavior seemed very odd."

"The man had been through a traumatic experience so that could explain his conduct." Ian leaned against the tree trunk. "It's not unusual for people to act dazed, confused, out-of-it after a devastating experience. The brain has to process the event."

"What about what he said to Vanessa, that she should pretend to be someone else if anyone came by to serve her a summons? Dr. Dodd told her not to speak to the police. He told her they had to stick together. If it was only an accident, why would he say such a thing?"

"He could have meant that he and the daughters had to support each other through the tragedy."

"Don't you think it's odd that he told Vanessa not to talk to the police." Claire brought up something else. "Dr. Dodd reported that he was in two different places when his wife fell. One time, he said he was resting on his bed on the second floor and another time, he said he was on the *first* floor when it happened."

Ian shrugged. "That could be chalked-up to the shock and brain fog."

Claire groaned. "You don't think it's anything to be concerned about then?"

"I didn't say that," Ian said. "There could be a whole lot to be concerned about. The police need to investigate." He gave Claire a look. "The *police*."

"I know you think we should keep our noses out of it." Lady came to rest in the shade with her owner and Claire scratched the dog's ears. "But Vanessa had a point. People might open up more with us than they would with an investigator. If some bit of news should come out of it, we'd go right to the police with the information."

"I can't stop you and Nicole, but I can offer you advice ... and warnings." Ian eyed Claire.

"And we'll gladly take your advice." Claire pushed at her drying bangs. "I'm looking at this as helping Vanessa. If we talk to a few people and

44

nothing seems amiss, then maybe she can let go of the thought that her father pushed his wife out the window. Maybe she'll be able to reconcile with her father. Maybe, over time, she can forgive his infidelity. She's lost her mother. It would be terrible to lose her father, too."

"Families can be shattered by things like this," Ian said. "I've seen it time and time again. When you and Nicole are talking to people, if things seem odd or shady or whatever, immediately extract yourselves from the situation. Don't press or challenge anyone. And report your findings to the police." Ian looked Claire in the eye. "Don't put yourselves at risk. Pay attention to what's going on. When you enter a room, look for two ways out. Watch the person's behavior for subtle changes. Desperate people can do desperate things. Don't dismiss your intuition."

"You're scaring me." Claire shuddered.

"Good. Keep on your toes. Trust no one. A situation can change in a flash."

"Want to come with us?" Claire gave a half-smile.

"I'm a detective. Wouldn't I make the interviewee clam up?"

"Oh, right," Claire kidded. "I forgot, you're a cop."

Bear rushed over and gave Ian a slurp on the

cheek causing the man to let out a hearty laugh. "Great, now I have dog slobber mixed with my sweat."

Claire smiled at the handsome Boston detective. "You'll be a hit with everyone at the police station."

"Speaking of which, I better get home so I can get ready for my shift." Ian high-fived Claire. "Nice run today. I'll meet you at 5am tomorrow to bike?"

Letting out a groan, Claire nodded. "So early. Why did I sign up for this mini-triathlon? In the future, stop me if I ever again suggest such a ridiculous thing."

"Next time, we'll train for an Iron-Man." Ian gave the dogs a pat and with a wave, headed down the hill.

The Corgis rested on the grass next to Claire and they watched the people and dogs walking by, college kids playing catch with a football, and others sunning themselves on the warm summer afternoon.

Lady let out a soft woof and Claire followed the dog's gaze to see two men sitting on a bench several hundred yards away. One of the men was small and wiry with jet black hair and seemed to be in his mid-fifties. The other man looked to be in his mid-sixties, carried a few extra pounds and had a good head of silver hair. He wore chinos and a long-sleeved button-down shirt. The older man had a serious expression and talked intently with his companion, occasionally gesturing to make a point. Claire thought his bearing and manner expressed agitation. She started to look away, but stopped and turned her attention back to the silver-haired man and her jaw almost dropped. It was Dr. Dodd.

Claire shifted a bit around the tree to keep an eye on the interaction and wished she was closer so she could hear the conversation. After several minutes, Claire decided to act, she took her phone from her arm band and discreetly took a photo of the two men, then she stood and strolled over towards the bench with the two Corgis walking behind her. When she approached the men, she acted surprised to see one of them. "Dr. Dodd? Hello."

The doctor looked up obviously unsure of who the young woman was. Bear and Lady held back and watched the doctor with suspicion.

"I'm Vanessa's friend. I'm very sorry for your loss."

"Oh, I see. Thank you." The doctor managed.

Claire turned to the doctor's companion and extended her hand. "I'm Claire Rollins."

The dark-haired man shook with her, but didn't introduce himself, disappointing Claire.

Unsure if the doctor's reported behavior on the night of the accident was due to the horror of his wife falling or from the guilt he felt for causing her death, Claire used a gentle tone when she asked, "How are you doing?" Dr. Dodd had several deep scratches on the side of his face.

The man wouldn't make eye contact with Claire. "As expected," he muttered.

"Vanessa and I made plans to meet this evening at your home. Is there anything I can bring by? A meal? Anything at all?"

"Nothing. Thank you." Dr. Dodd adjusted his position on the bench to better face the man he was with, subtly indicating to Claire that he wanted her exchange with him to end.

"I'll see you tonight." Claire nodded at the two men and started away, tension squeezing her muscles. *Whether you want to see me or not.*

6

The Dodd's six-thousand square foot home had high ceilings, gleaming wood floors, woven carpets of muted colors, and rooms that looked like an expensive designer had been given free rein and access to an unlimited bank account. Luxurious furnishings, chandeliers, and expensive art work decorated every room that Vanessa walked Claire and Nicole through to the kitchen.

"What a beautiful kitchen." Claire stared at the walls of cherry cabinets, the massive granite countertops, and the high-end appliances. A fireplace stood on the wall of the dining nook. 'Nook' wasn't a word Claire would use to describe the enormous space.

"My parents added this room and the family room when I was in high school. The kitchen was recently updated." Vanessa gestured to the round glass table. "Have a seat. My father's at a meeting so we have some time to talk before he gets home. I'll go get Maddy."

Claire couldn't imagine growing up in such a place. Despite her mother working two jobs, they were always only one paycheck away from losing their apartment. Even though her late husband had been a wealthy businessman, Claire never quite got used to having the sense of stability that came with financial security. "Did you grow up in a house like this?" Claire whispered to her friend.

Nicole snorted. "I grew up on the *other* side of town."

Maddy and Vanessa came into the kitchen and sat down at the table. Maddy looked pretty, she had done her makeup and styled her hair, yet the spark Claire had seen in the young woman when she met her was gone. Maddy shrank into herself and her eyes flicked about the room as she clutched her hands together in her lap. The sadness Maddy gave off pulled at Claire's heart.

Nicole reached across the table and took Maddy's hand. "I've been thinking of you."

Maddy nodded. The edges of her eyelids were tinged red and her eyes were bloodshot.

"My father will be home soon," Vanessa said. "I thought we could talk before he gets back."

Claire made eye contact with Vanessa and then glanced at Maddy.

"You can speak freely in front of my sister. We've talked about everything. We feel the same way about what's been going on."

Claire said, "I ran into your father today on the Boston Common. He was sitting on a bench talking to a man."

"Was he?" Vanessa's eyes narrowed. "What did the man look like?"

Claire reported on the man's appearance and how he seemed to deliberately avoid telling her his name.

"I wonder what that was about," Vanessa thought out loud.

"I took a picture of them." Claire reached for her phone and pulled up the photograph. "Here it is. It's a little grainy."

Vanessa peered at the picture and handed the phone back to Claire. "I don't know him. I don't think I've ever seen him before."

Nicole wanted to bring Maddy into the conversation. "What are you thinking about the accident?"

Maddy shrugged a shoulder. "I don't know. I'm not sure what to think. I don't think it was an accident though."

"Can you tell us what happened when you arrived home from the Opera House?" Claire asked trying to get the young woman talking.

Maddy blinked fast several times. "I walked up to the house. It was dark. I was going up to the front porch and I saw the door was open. I looked to both sides of the porch thinking maybe Mom or Dad came outside for something for a minute. No one was around. I got a little nervous. I stood at the door and pushed it all the way open and called for my parents. I found Dad in his office and asked what was wrong. He looked kind of ... his eyes were wild, they were big and darting around. Dad was pacing fast, up and down in front of his desk. He had his phone in his hand and Mom's raincoat over his arm. He had some blood on the side of his face. I asked him again what was wrong ... he just glanced at me, kept pacing. He kept checking his phone like he was waiting for a call." Tears started in Maddy's eyes. "I started to panic. He was acting so weird. I grabbed his arm. I think I screamed at him to tell me what was wrong." She looked down and shook her head. "He pulled his arm away and kept pacing. I ran out of the room calling for Mom. I ran through the downstairs rooms looking for her and then I ran upstairs to the bedrooms. I couldn't find her." Maddy's voice hitched with emotion and Vanessa put her arm over her sister's shoulders.

Maddy took in a raspy breath. "I didn't know what to do. I raced up the stairs to the third floor. Mom never goes up there, but I didn't know what else to do. I had to find her. Dad was acting so strange, it scared me."

"What happened when you went to the third floor?" Nicole asked.

"When I was going through the rooms, I felt cool air so I ran to the bedroom thinking Mom must be in there. She must have opened the window. I felt a rush of relief that she was in there." Maddy bit her lip. "When I went in the room, no one was there. The window. There was some glass on the floor. The window screen was missing. I walked over and looked out." The young woman's hand flew to cover her eyes and she whispered. "Mom. Mom was on the ground."

Claire's heart ached from Maddy's grief and

misery and she had to bite the inside of her cheek to keep her own tears from falling.

After giving the girl a few minutes to collect herself, Nicole asked, "Then you went outside?"

"Uh-huh. I ran down the stairs and out the front door to the side of the house. Mom was crumpled on the ground. She had blood.... I grabbed her hand and talked to her. She didn't open her eyes, but I could hear her breathing. It was sort of raggedy, but she was breathing. I reached for my shoulder bag to get my phone and I realized I left it inside, but then I heard the sirens. Dad must have called them. I thought they'd never get here."

"You stayed with your mother until the emergency personnel showed up?" Claire asked.

Maddy gave a nod.

"Did your father come out?"

"I don't think so. Not right away anyway. Lorraine was here. She helped me. She kept talking to Mom."

"Did your mother respond or open her eyes?" Claire questioned.

"She moaned a little, but that was all." Maddy swallowed. "I remember Dad *did* come out when Lorraine was with me. He put the raincoat over Mom. He and Lorraine said some things to each other. I wasn't paying attention. Then the EMTs showed up."

"Did your father talk to your mother? Did he say anything to her?" Nicole asked.

"No, he didn't. He didn't kneel down or anything." Maddy looked from person to person and her voice hardened. "Why didn't he?"

Vanessa squeezed her sister's hand and gave a shrug.

"Was anyone else here in the house that night?" Claire asked.

Maddy shook her head. "Just Dad. Vanessa was on the way to New York. No one else lives here."

"What about a family friend? A household helper?"

Maddy thought for a moment staring blankly at the table. "No."

"Did you see any signs of a struggle?"

Maddy lifted her head and made eye contact with Claire. "A struggle? No." The young woman's forehead creased. "Wait. There was a brush on the floor in my parents' room, and a book, too." Her eyes got wide. "The chair at the vanity wasn't in its place."

Vanessa's eyes locked on her sister.

Claire's heart raced. Could those things be a sign of a fight? "What do you mean about the chair?"

"My mom always pushes the chair in when she's done at the vanity." Maddy cocked her head. "The chair was next to the wall near the bed. She never puts it there."

Thoughts swirled in Claire's brain. Did someone rush around trying to right things that were tipped over from a struggle? Is that why Dr. Dodd wasn't outside with his wife? Is that the reason Maddy found him in his office pacing around?

"Think back." Claire leaned forward. "Did anything else seem off in the house?"

"I don't think so," Maddy said slowly.

"Tell them what you saw in the third floor bedroom," Vanessa suggested.

"When I was about to go into the bedroom, there was something on the woodwork. It looked like part of a handprint, in blood."

Anxiety flashed through Claire's body. "Blood was on the woodwork? On the door casing?"

Maddy nodded and lifted her hand. "The print is of these three fingers." She folded down her thumb and pinky leaving the index, middle, and ring fingers standing up. "The mark looks sort of smeared like someone's hand was moving when it touched the wood."

Vanessa got up from her seat. "It's still there.

We'll take you up to the third floor before Dad gets home. You can see the mark on the woodwork and the window Mom fell from."

The four climbed the stairs to the third floor and walked down a hallway.

"Here's the room." Vanessa pointed. "The police have been all over the place a million times so it doesn't matter if you touch anything. Here's the spot on the woodwork." She indicated a dark, small, dried bloody smear about half-way up the door frame.

Claire and Nicole leaned forward to get a better look.

"This definitely wasn't here before the night of the accident?" Claire asked.

"Well, I don't know, for sure." Vanessa stared at the spot. "We never come up here. I suppose it could have been. Do you think the police would be able to date it?"

"I have no idea." Claire straightened. "Can you tell whose print it is? From the size?"

"I initially thought it was Mom's, but because of the smearing, I can't be sure. Maddy and I talked about it and we just don't know." Vanessa looked around for her sister and saw her standing by the window looking out. The glass had already been replaced.

"The window's been fixed?" Nicole asked.

"Dad didn't waste any time." Vanessa's voice held a tone of contempt. She walked across the room. "Maddy?"

Maddy didn't turn, she just kept staring out.

Vanessa looked from Claire to Nicole and then stepped close to her sister and put her hand on the girl's arm. "Why don't you come away from the window."

Claire expected to see tears on the young woman's cheeks when she shifted her position to face her sister, but Maddy's face was dry.

"You know ... I remember something," Maddy spoke slowly. "I think someone was in the yard. I think the person went into the trees. Whoever it was must have seen Mom fall."

7

"What do you mean? Someone was in the yard?" Vanessa asked with a tone of urgency.

"I think so." Maddy ran her hand over her hair. "The window was broken, there was some glass on the floor. I remember how it crunched when I walked over it. My heart was pounding. I was afraid to look, but I kind of inched to the window and looked down. I saw Mom. At first, I wasn't sure if it was a person or not. Something moved, over there." Maddy pointed to the side yard toward the back and left of the house. "I think someone was standing there and then they moved into the trees."

"Are you sure someone was there?" Vanessa asked.

"No," Maddy said weakly. "But I saw movement and then whatever it was that moved was gone."

"Could it have been the wind moving some branches?" Claire peered out the window.

"I don't think so. The movement was close to the ground. Like feet moving. It seemed like a shadow, but then it didn't." Maddy placed her hand on the side of her face.

Vanessa checked her watch. "I think we should go downstairs. Dad will be home soon and I don't want him to find us up here."

As soon as the young women descended the stairs and headed for the kitchen, Dr. Dodd came in from the garage. His head snapped up when he heard the four voices and he looked wide-eyed from girl to girl.

"Hello, Dad." There was no warmth in Vanessa's voice as she pulled herself up to full height. "You remember Nicole. And this is Claire, a friend of Nicole's."

Dr. Dodd nodded to the guests. His face seemed tense and his body language appeared stiff and uncomfortable.

"I met you at the Common today," Claire reminded the man.

"Yes." Dr. Dodd shifted his eyes around the room

like he was looking for an escape route. "I'm going to my office," he said before scurrying out of the room.

"This is the odd behavior I told you about." Vanessa kept her voice low in case her father came back into the room. "It isn't actually what he says, it's the whole thing. He acts nervous, withdrawn, he doesn't want to spend time around people. He just wants to be alone. Whenever he's at home, he barricades himself in his office."

"You've tried to talk to him?" Nicole asked.

"I'll go in the office and try to get him to talk," Vanessa said.

Maddy crossed her arms over her chest. "I don't try to talk to him."

Vanessa went on. "When I go in to talk to him, he acts so busy like he's working feverishly. I ask him something and he looks at me blankly like I'm speaking a foreign language. If he answers, he answers evasively. He often contradicts himself. Like I told you, he said he was in bed on the second floor when Mom fell and another time he told me he was in the kitchen."

"Isn't that a sign of trauma?" Claire asked. "Like his mind isn't working right because of what he's been through?"

"It can be a sign of stress." Vanessa frowned. "He

can't keep his story straight. He asks us to lie for him. He asked me to pretend to be someone else so I couldn't be served a summons."

"What was he like before the accident happened?" Nicole asked.

Vanessa suddenly looked exhausted. "He was pleasant, he tried to be friendly. There was always a little uneasiness when we were all together ... because of the affair, but we managed okay. Maddy and I held resentment towards him for what he'd done to Mom ... but we tried to keep it in check."

Claire asked, "Did your father ever explain why he had blood and scratches on his face?"

"When I first asked him, he wouldn't answer," Vanessa said. "When I asked the same question on another day, he said he and Mom had an argument that night. He said she struck him."

"What were they arguing about?" Nicole questioned. "Did he tell you?"

"He was evasive ... his newest quality," Vanessa said sarcastically. "He mumbled that their arguing wasn't anything new. When I pressed for more details, he clammed up." She glanced down the hall. "I want us all to go into his office and talk to him. See if we can get anything new from him."

Nicole's face screwed up. "Do you think that's a

good idea? If he won't talk to you, he sure won't talk to us."

"Maddy and I talked about it." Vanessa turned to her sister. "We think she should stay out of it. The three of us will go in and start a conversation."

"That will seem weird." The corners of Nicole's lips pulled down. "If the three of us go in there asking questions, he'll think it's some kind of inquisition. He'll never talk."

Claire spoke up. "What if we make some tea or bring in some wine? We could bring in cookies or whatever. You can say that we don't want him to be alone, we could chat and see where it leads."

Vanessa's face brightened. "Perfect." She and Maddy scurried around the kitchen getting out a tray, wine glasses, a bottle of wine, some cheese and crackers.

Vanessa, Claire, and Nicole carried the items to the office where Vanessa knocked and opened the door. "We thought you might like a glass of wine."

Dr. Dodd sat behind his desk and a look of horror washed over his face. "No, thank you. I'm very busy."

Claire and Nicole took a seat on the small sofa near the desk. Vanessa poured the wine and passed around glasses ignoring her father's protestations. "We'll only stay for a little while."

"It was a beautiful day on the Common today," Claire smiled.

Dr. Dodd looked at Claire as if he had no idea what she was saying.

"You walked over from the hospital?" Vanessa asked. "Who were you with?"

The man sat silently in his chair.

"Dad. Who did you go to the Common with today?" Vanessa wasn't about to give up.

"Someone from the hospital," the doctor said absent-mindedly.

"A doctor?"

Dr. Dodd shook his head. "What? No."

"How do you know him then?"

"He's on staff. Where's Maddy?" The doctor looked over to the door. "She's been sleeping a lot lately. Is she okay?"

"She's upset," Vanessa said through gritted teeth.

"Yes," Dr. Dodd's comment seemed to slip quietly into the air.

Nicole offered her condolences and the man made eye contact with her, but said nothing.

Claire said, "It's a very trying time. It's hard to

think straight at a time like this. My husband passed away from a heart attack two years ago."

Vanessa looked over at Claire with an expression of surprise.

"It's still difficult to believe that he's gone. I spent hours and hours wondering if there was something I could have done that might have prevented his death. Should I have noticed something? Was he not feeling well? Was he fatigued? Did anything at all seem off?" Claire shook her head. "Someone told me it's natural to second guess our actions after someone we love passes away, to blame ourselves for not being more vigilant." Claire held the doctor's eyes. "Vanessa said that Mrs. Dodd hardly ever used the third floor. Do you know why she was up there?"

"I have no idea." The doctor stood up and scrambled around from behind the desk. As he made his way to the door, Claire stood and extended her hand to him. "I'm very sorry if I said something to upset you."

Dodd took Claire's hand for a brief moment and then disappeared out the door. Claire and Nicole exchanged a look.

"Sorry this didn't work," Claire said to Vanessa.

"Did your husband really pass away?" Vanessa asked.

Claire gave a nod.

"God, I'm sorry." Vanessa gave Claire a hug. "Don't worry that our chat ended so soon. He wouldn't have told us anything anyway. Let's get out of here." Vanessa picked up the wine bottle and started for the hall. "Just leave the glasses. The housekeeper will be in tomorrow morning."

Claire and Nicole put the glasses on the tray despite Vanessa's suggestion to leave them on the desk. Nicole lifted the tray and leaned closer to her friend. "Did you feel anything when you shook the doctor's hand?"

"Yes," Claire whispered and took a quick glance to the doorway. "Dr. Dodd has a firm idea why his wife was on the third floor."

Nicole's eyes went wide. "You and that intuition of yours are amazing. Were you able to pick up on what he knows about the *reason* his wife was up there?"

"Guess what." Claire frowned. "I'm not *that* amazing."

8
_____

Claire sat with Augustus at the little table in Tony's shop. Bear and Lady followed Tony from the front of the deli to the store room in back keeping him company as he did his work. A few days a week, the dogs stayed with Tony at the small market in Adamsburg Square while Claire worked at Nicole's chocolate shop. There was a small garden off the store room where the dogs liked to spend part of the day.

Sipping her hot tea, Claire told Augustus the latest news in the Grace Dodd case.

Tony came out of the back room carrying a box of cheese and headed to the deli case. "Don't tell anything when I'm in the back. I can't hear what you're saying."

67

Claire repeated what she'd just reported to Augustus.

Tony stepped from behind the counter wiping his hands on his white apron. "The man's behavior is odd. I hope he's getting some counseling. The way he's acting could give people the idea he's guilty."

"I think he knows more than he's telling." In fact, Claire was sure of this after shaking hands with the man last night, but she couldn't tell Tony and Augustus that she had strong *intuition*.

"I feel bad for the guy." Tony sat at the table. "What a heck of a mess."

Augustus adjusted his bow tie. "It can look bad for the man. He had an affair, perhaps it was ongoing. Vanessa reports that her parents argued about it. Physical violence may have taken place during the arguments. Both probably felt ashamed that their lives were not what they'd hoped they would be. Mrs. Dodd felt betrayed by her husband. Something in the husband compelled him to engage in an affair."

"He had the stupid affair with a high-profile *married* woman." Tony shook his head. "Not very discreet of either of them. Someone would've found them out eventually."

"Can investigators determine how old the blood

is that's on the woodwork on the third floor?" Claire asked Augustus.

"It's possible, but it is difficult. I'd guess nothing definitive will come from trying to date the blood."

Claire's shoulders sagged with disappointment, but then she said, "Even if it's not dated, the blood indicates a fight, doesn't it? If someone was up there and got hurt, they'd clean the blood off the door frame. They wouldn't leave it there. So it makes me think the blood is pretty new."

"Good point." Tony nodded.

"What about the housekeeper?" Augustus asked. "Vanessa mentioned that you could leave the wine glasses in Dr. Dodd's office. The family employs outside help. It might be useful to interview the housekeeper and whoever else works for the Dodds. A gardener, perhaps?"

Bear let out a low woof.

Tony crossed his big arms over his chest. "What about this business of Maddy suddenly remembering someone moving around in the yard that night?"

Claire looked at Tony. "You think she's mistaken?"

"Why did she remember it all of a sudden?"

Augustus set his mug onto the table. "It's not

unusual. The trauma and stress of the event ... losing a loved one suddenly and unexpectedly ... this can cause the brain to slow down. The horror of what has happened can keep people from recalling details."

"Can it also cause people to recall things that didn't happen?" Tony narrowed his eyes. "Can it cause people to distort what they've seen?"

"What are you getting at?" Claire asked.

"Maybe the girl saw something in the yard. It could have been a raccoon or whatever. The girl sees the movement, doesn't see anything clearly, and then fills in the blanks later assuming it was a person who was in the yard."

"Huh, good point," Claire said. "Maybe you should sell this deli and become an investigator."

Tony rolled his eyes. "It's common sense, Blondie."

"It's a good point." Claire grinned at the man. "So I'm going to talk to the neighbor and I'll ask about the housekeeping staff, and maybe I'll talk to them, too."

"Have Vanessa and her sister considered the possibility of an intruder?" Augustus asked.

With wide eyes, Claire turned to the retired judge. "An intruder? I don't think that's come up at all. Dr. Dodd was at home. Wouldn't he know if an intruder broke into the house?"

"Would he?" Augustus asked. "Dr. Dodd said, in one of his claims anyway, that he was on the second floor in bed resting from a headache. He'd taken a sleeping pill. Someone could have broken into the house while he was asleep. Mrs. Dodd may have seen the person and ran to the third floor trying to escape him. She was caught, a fight ensued, and she was pushed from the window."

Claire stared at the man. "Wouldn't there be signs of an intruder? Wouldn't the police suspect such a thing?"

"It's a consideration, that's all."

"Here's another consideration." Tony reached down to scratch Lady's ears. "Don't jump down my throat when I say this."

A shiver of unease ran over Claire's skin.

"You don't know this family well at all. What about the sisters?"

"What about them?" Claire's eyebrow raised.

Tony didn't answer for a few moments. "How do you know one of them didn't push the woman?"

Her heart pounding double-time, Claire's head swam at the suggestion. Her immediate response was to defend Vanessa and Maddy, but honestly, she didn't know them at all. "Vanessa was on a train to New York when it happened. Maddy was on the commuter rail train heading home when it happened."

"So they say." Tony made eye contact with Claire.

Claire clutched the sides of her chair.

"How do you know they were on those trains?" Tony pressed.

"Tony has a point," Augustus said. "It is thought that the incident happened while the sisters were on the trains. What if one, or both, took a cab to the house? Taking a cab may have allowed them to arrive in time to commit the crime, leave, and then return at the times the trains would have deposited them."

Tony said, "Vanessa might be making a fuss about her father to make him look like the guilty one. Maddy might tell you she saw someone in the yard to move suspicion onto some mystery person."

Claire rested her head in her palm and groaned. "My God. I didn't think of any of this."

Tony stood up to wait on a customer. "That's why we're here, Blondie. To keep you on the right track."

With a frown, Claire looked sheepishly to Augustus. "I didn't think of any of those things."

Augustus patted the woman's hand. "You're

young. You look for the good in people. We have seen a lot in our old lives. You aren't as jaded as Tony and I have become. Hold on to your trust and optimism, Claire. It is a needed commodity in this world."

"But I almost overlooked something."

"You would have considered all of the possibilities eventually." Augustus winked. "Tony and I just brought it to your attention a bit sooner. The young women are most likely innocent. Just remember that on occasion, things are not as they seem."

Augustus's words sent a chill along Claire's back. "I'll look into the timelines of the train schedules. Maybe Nicole and I will take a cab from the Opera House to Greendale one of these days to see how long it takes to get from the city to the house."

"Remember to take the cab on the same day of the week and the same time of evening that matches the circumstances on the night of the event."

Claire nodded. "We will." A terrible feeling slid through her body at the thought that Vanessa or Maddy could have pushed their mother from the window and that she and Nicole were being played by one of them. She wanted to talk to Nicole about the possibility. Another thought popped into her head. "What about the woman Dr. Dodd was having an affair with? Maybe she came to confront Mrs. Dodd to get her to agree to a divorce. Then she and Dr. Dodd would be free to get married. The woman and Mrs. Dodd might have fought."

"Another possibility." Augustus took a swallow of his coffee. "The police are probably looking into all of this."

Claire tilted her head in question. "You think Nicole and I should stay out of it?"

"I did not say that." Augustus shook his head. "You and Nicole are trying to help a friend of Nicole's. In my experience, ordinary citizens often uncover something that had been overlooked or went unseen and a case is solved. From the last incident you were involved in, it is clear that some people will do anything for money or power or to satisfy their selfish desires." Augustus looked straight into Claire's eyes. "In cases such as these, vigilance is called for. Don't let down your guard."

Claire nodded and tried to lighten the mood. "In other words, look both ways before I cross the street."

"Look before you leap," Augustus added.

"Oh, I need to get to the chocolate shop." Claire leapt to her feet, cleared away her used tea mug, and gave each Corgi a pat. "I'll see you tomorrow," she told Augustus with a smile. "Thanks for the advice."

Claire called goodbye to Tony who was behind the deli case. "See you later today."

When she stepped outside into the hot summer air and hurried down the brick walkway to the North End, a shiver like a cold finger of warning traced down Claire's back from the conversation she'd just had with Tony and Augustus. The only problem was she couldn't tell what part of the discussion warranted the danger sign.

9

———

Claire and Nicole sat on sofas in Lorraine Hale's sunroom at the back of her house across the street from the Dodd residence. The three walls of glass doors were open to allow the breeze to pass through and the room was perfectly situated to make the most of the view of the professionally landscaped backyard. Cookies, fruit, iced tea, and sparkling water sat on the coffee table.

Lorraine, a slender woman with short blond hair and bright blue eyes, sat across from the young women with her hands in her lap.

"Thank you for meeting with us." Claire had worked for years as a corporate attorney and met her late husband while employed at his company. After Teddy passed away, she needed a change and gave up her career, moved to Boston, and being a talented amateur baker decided to apply for the position at Nicole's chocolate shop. Even though Claire had limited knowledge of criminal investigation, Vanessa told Lorraine that she'd retained Claire to do some preliminary inquiries about the accident in order to represent the family's best interests.

"We're gathering some information about what happened to Grace Dodd so that the family has a clear understanding of the accident," Claire told Lorraine.

"I see," Lorraine gave a nod. "I hope I can help. I can't believe Grace is gone. Every time I'm in the front yard or on the porch and I look over at her house, I have to shake myself. It all seems like a bad dream."

"Have you talked with Dr. Dodd since the accident?"

"I brought over a few meals to Ronald the other evening. If he didn't want them, I thought Maddy might eat them." Lorraine reached for her glass of seltzer. "Ronald wasn't very talkative. I suppose that's understandable."

"Can you tell us about your friendship with the Dodds?" Nicole asked.

"We were friends for, oh ... twenty years. Maybe a little longer." Lorraine paused and took a deep breath. "You don't realize how much a person means to you until they're gone." She took another swallow from her glass. "Grace and I hit it off right away when my husband and I moved to the neighborhood. Vanessa and my son were about the same age. It was nice to be able to help each other out watching the kids if one of us had an errand or a doctor's appointment." A wistful look passed over the woman's face. "Time flies."

"Did you get together as couples?" Claire asked.

"We did. We'd go to a show or to the symphony together. We'd take turns having dinner together once a month. Our husbands golfed occasionally, we'd all play tennis."

"Did you or your husband notice a change in Grace or Ronald recently?"

Lorraine seemed to bite the inside of her lower lip. "We didn't socialize as much as we used to."

"Did you still see the Dodds?" Nicole questioned.

"I saw Grace quite a lot. Ronald was often busy. We hadn't been together as couples for some time."

Claire looked pointedly at Lorraine. "Vanessa told us about the marital problems."

"Did she?" Lorraine's eyebrows went up and she nodded. "Well. Ronald was unfaithful. Grace took it hard."

"Can you tell us more?" Nicole encouraged the woman. "They were still together. They wanted to work it out?"

"Grace wanted to file for divorce right away, but after giving it some thought, she decided to wait. She and Ronald had been married for over forty years. Grace didn't want to throw it all away without thinking things through first."

"She was willing to forgive the transgression?" Claire asked.

"No," Lorraine almost shouted. "She certainly was not. She felt the betrayal to be something she would never be able to forgive. Grace felt Ronald had changed too much, she didn't think she would ever be able to trust him again. She said he wasn't the man she'd married and lived with for so many years. Grace said sometimes she didn't know him at all."

"Then why did she want to wait to file for divorce?" Nicole tilted her head in question.

"Grace wanted to be sure the financials were in

order so she went to an attorney to get things worked out before she left Ronald."

"Was she close to filing for divorce?" Claire thought if Ronald knew his wife was going to divorce him soon, it could have provoked an argument between them.

"It would have been filed over the next couple of weeks."

"Grace confided in you," Nicole said. "Did she explain how she thought Ronald had changed?"

"Grace said he'd become distant. He didn't take any interest in their family life. Ronald always had excuses to be somewhere else. I'm sure he loves the girls, but his priorities seem to have shifted." Lorraine's face darkened. "We all know what took up his time."

"Do you know who Ronald was having the affair with?" Nicole asked.

"I know who she is. A married woman, too." Lorraine huffed. "They deserve each other."

"Did the woman ever come to the Dodd's house?"

Lorraine reacted as if she'd been struck. "My God, I certainly hope not."

"How do you feel about Dr. Dodd?" Claire asked.

"Would you and your husband keep up the friendship?"

"My friendship was with Grace. I know it's a terrible thing to say, but I don't care what happens to Ronald. He's not the man I thought he was. I guess he hid his real self for years. Maybe I never knew him at all." A cloud seemed to descend over Lorraine.

"Can you tell us if the Dodd's employed any household help?" Claire asked even though she had been told the Dodds had a domestic employee.

"They have a housekeeper. She comes three to five days a week to clean, make a light meal if they need something."

"Has the person worked for them for a long time?"

"A few years, at least."

"Do you know her name?"

"Um," Lorraine thought about it, but couldn't come up with the information. "She's short, stocky, about mid-fifties. Vanessa could tell you the woman's name."

"What about a gardener or a landscaper?" Nicole questioned.

"We use the same company. The man spends two days a week here and two days at the Dodd's. He mows, takes care of the flowers and the grass, mulches the beds, things like that. His name is Warren. Warren King."

"Has he worked for you for a long time?"

"A couple of years."

"I hate to ask the question," Claire began, "but how would you describe Grace's mental state?"

Lorraine's eyes widened. "There was nothing wrong with Grace. She still worked, she was successful. If I had to describe her recent state with one word, then I'd choose angry. Grace tried to raise her daughters to be good people, she loved those girls. She worked hard to do well in her career. She worked at her marriage. Ronald's transgression was a slap in Grace's face. She came to think of Ronald as weak, selfish. Grace began to despise him. She was a strong woman. If you're asking if she was down, then yes, she was. If you're asking if she was disappointed and heartbroken, yes, she was. If you're asking me if Grace had given up hope and was suicidal, I'd tell you absolutely not. She wanted to rid her life of Ronald's foolishness. She wanted to move on. Grace would never have done anything that would take her from her daughters. Never. Those girls were the light of her life."

"Can you think of anyone who might have wished Grace ill?"

Lorraine's mouth dropped open. "Are you thinking this *isn't* some freak accident? Do you think someone pushed Grace?"

Claire leaned forward. "Mrs. Hale, did you happen to see anyone around the Dodd's house that day or night? Think back. Was there anything unusual that day? Someone in the neighborhood who looked out of place? Anything at all that seemed like nothing, but under the circumstances could be a clue to what happened to your friend?"

Flustered by the questions, Lorraine's face reddened and her eyes darted around the room. "I don't know. I was at home most of the day, but my husband and I went out to dinner. When we got home, I read in the den. That's where I was when I heard Maddy screaming. I didn't notice anything that seemed unusual." The woman's hand brushed over her eyes. "Do you think foul play was involved? I thought maybe Grace opened the window, lost her balance and fell." Lorraine's breathing rate increased. "You think she was pushed? My God, was it Ronald? Did they fight? Did he push her?"

Claire could see that Lorraine's fluster was quickly turning into panic. "We don't know anything at all. It could certainly have been an accident, but because of the unusual circumstances, the family wants to be sure every base is covered."

"When you say family, do you mean Vanessa and Maddy only?"

"Yes," Claire nodded. "We're representing Vanessa and Maddy's interests."

Lorraine seemed to relax slightly. "Good. That's good. Grace was a real advocate for the girls. I'm glad to see that they are stepping up and taking care of things."

Nicole asked, "How do you mean that Grace was an advocate for Vanessa and Maddy?"

"The girls were Grace's main focus in life. Grace and Ronald have a very large estate. Grace was working to make sure the estate would go to the girls, not some woman Ronald might end up marrying." Lorraine rubbed at her temple. "The girls had a monthly allowance. Grace wanted to be sure that they had what they needed. She always said how difficult it was for young people to get started in life so she and Ronald had set up an allowance to help them out. Grace was adamant that this would continue if she filed for divorce. She told me that Ronald wanted to end the financial help to the girls."

Claire's heart rate sped up. "Was the allowance continuing?"

"I'm not sure."

Nicole asked, "Why did Ronald want it to end?"

"Ronald wanted it to end because he wanted to protect his *own* interests. Grace was sure he was funneling money to an off-shore account. She didn't want his antics to impact the girls."

Nicole raised an eyebrow. "Do you know how much money was involved in helping the daughters?"

Lorraine hesitated for a moment. "I don't think Grace would have minded if I tell you since you've been hired to look out for the girls. Vanessa and Maddy each got one hundred thousand dollars a year."

Claire and Nicole exchanged a quick look of surprise.

Claire made sure her voice remained calm and even. "I can understand that the parents might have argued about it. It is a substantial amount of money."

"Grace wanted the money to go to the girls and not into Ronald's secret bank account." Lorraine shook her head. "It's so very difficult to believe how things have worked out ... Grace is gone, Ronald is ...

I don't even know what to say about Ronald and what he's become. How I wish things could go back to the way they were." Lorraine sighed and looked from Claire to Nicole. "I'm so very glad you're helping Vanessa and Maddy. Don't let Ronald take their mother's money from them. Please, look out for the girls."

10

Claire hurried over the sidewalk to get to the chocolate shop in time for her shift and as she rounded the corner, she almost plowed right into Robby who was hurrying to work just as quickly as she was. They chuckled when they saw who they nearly collided with. Robby held the door and Claire stepped out of the heat and into the cool air of the café.

"Are you in any more upcoming musicals? I can't wait to go again."

"I think I have a new fan," Robby joked.

"You definitely do. You're fabulous. I think I'm going to be your manager."

"I don't pay much."

Claire winked. "You will when I make you rich

and famous."

"Do you have any experience?"

"None, but I'm a fast learner."

"I think I'll pass." Robby kidded. "You're probably a better baker than a manager."

They joined Nicole in the back room to prepare more of the day's bakery items and the back and forth banter between them filled each one with energy and good cheer. Customers streamed in and out of the shop all morning and the three workers could barely keep up.

Robby carried out a tray of sweets to replenish the bakery cases. "You need to hire more help. It's more than we can handle."

"I don't know." Nicole wiped down the counters and the tabletops. "I'm not sure I can afford another employee. Maybe I'll dock your salary so I can pay for additional help."

"Cut my pay, huh? It might be time to give my notice."

Nicole laughed. "Don't you dare."

When Robby headed to the back room, Claire sidled up to Nicole. "We need to talk about what Tony and Augustus brought up in the deli yesterday. I never considered those things." They discussed what the men had said about a possible intruder or that Vanessa and Maddy might have had something to do with Grace Dodd's accident. "I told you what they said about Maddy ... she could have imagined a person in the yard when her mother fell."

Nicole's face took on more and more of an alarmed look. "I don't want to admit it, but all of those things *are* possible and as much as I'm horrified by it, we really can't dismiss any of it, can we? I'll be devastated if Vanessa or Maddy are involved." Placing clean dishes on the shelves over the counters, she asked, "How can we figure out if Vanessa and Maddy were on the trains they said they were on?"

Claire cut slices into an enormous chocolate mousse cake. "I don't think we can, but we can look up the times the trains run. We could see how long it takes for the commuter rail train to get to Greendale from the city. That would tell us if Maddy could have been home in time to play a part in the incident. We can also check to see if there really is a train back to Boston when Vanessa said she changed trains to return to the city."

Nicole leaned back against the counter. "If Vanessa pushed her mother from the window, why would she ask us to interview people?"

"It could be she's trying to deflect attention to

another suspect. She acts outraged and says things that make her father look bad. She could be trying to throw people off her trail."

Nicole groaned. "I've just reconnected with Vanessa. I hadn't seen her for years. How awful it would be to renew a friendship with her only to discover she's a murderer."

"We're checking everything so we can eliminate suspects. I'm sure Vanessa is innocent of any wrongdoing, but we'd be remiss if we didn't look into it. Don't the police always look at family members first? It's standard operating procedure, isn't it? In order to cross them off the list?"

"You'll have to ask Ian. I don't know anything." Nicole gave Claire the eye. "What about your intuition? Can you eliminate someone by shaking hands with them?"

Claire let out a sigh. "I don't think so. I can pick up on deceit or some foreboding, but not all the time. Since I've been meeting Tessa, I feel like I don't pick up on things as easily as I did before." Claire had met Tessa, a part-time psychic and intuit, in the chocolate shop when she'd come in one day for a coffee and dessert. Tessa was teaching Claire how to control her impulses and intuition so that Claire was in charge of the skill and the skill wasn't in control of her. When her abilities started to strongly manifest during the previous month, the whole thing frightened Claire. She wanted to be able to stop random feelings from percolating up. She wanted to be able to employ her skill when *she* wanted to use it.

"Why is that happening? Your skill isn't going away, is it?" Nicole poured a cup of tea for herself.

"Tessa said it happens sometimes when a person is learning to filter out unwanted impressions. She said the skill should return to normal eventually."

"Oh, great," Nicole said. "Now we're on our own with only our normal abilities. I don't think it will be enough."

Claire smiled. "We're pretty smart and we're good at reading people. I think we'll be okay."

Nicole held her mug in her two hands and made a face. "If you didn't have your witchy powers, we wouldn't have figured out half of what we did on that last case. We might have gotten killed."

"Please don't call them *witchy powers*." Claire shuddered. "It's nothing like that. It's being open to someone's feelings. I bet you could do it, if you tried."

"No, I could not." Nicole shook her head. "And it's definitely more than being open to feelings. It's … *witchy*."

Robby brought out another tray of chocolates from the back room. "Who's a witch?"

"Claire," Nicole said with a straight-face.

"Oh, yeah, I know." Robby placed the chocolates in the display case.

Claire put a hand on her hip. "What's that supposed to mean?"

Straightening up, Robby held a chocolate between his thumb and index finger and looked at Nicole. "This one has a dent in it. Can I eat it?"

Nicole narrowed her eyes. "Did you put the dent in it?"

"Absolutely not."

"Go ahead then."

"When am I ever a witch around you?" Claire demanded.

Robby put the whole sweet into his mouth and mumbled, "Not that kind of witch. You know, the other kind."

Claire glared at the young man. "What are you talking about?"

Swallowing the chocolate, Robby cleared his throat. "Last month, Nicole made you and I hold hands so you could try to sense something from me. Remember? Well, you did sense something. When we left the shop that day, you wished me good luck on the try-out."

Claire continued to stare.

"I never told anyone about that try-out." Robby stared back at Claire. "No one. But, you knew."

"I ... I...." Claire blustered.

"You don't need to make up some silly story to deny it." Robby started for the work room. "It's no big deal. My grandmother could do stuff like that." He chuckled. "We all called her 'Witchy Wynonna.' Hmm. Maybe I'll start calling you 'Clairvoyant Claire.'"

Claire turned to Nicole with a pale face. "Look what you've done."

With a wicked smile, Nicole busied herself with the cash register. "Clairvoyant Claire has a nice ring to it."

"News flash." Robby stuck his head out from the back room. "I just got an alert on my phone. State Representative Victoria Lowe has been found dead in her Boston townhouse. Whoever she is." He retreated back into the work room.

Nicole and Claire looked at each other with open mouths.

"Victoria Lowe." Claire's heart pounded like a hammer.

"Dr. Dodd's lover." Nicole's hand flew to her chest as she called to Robby. "What was the cause of death?"

"It didn't say," Robby spoke from the back room.

"I'll text Ian," Claire said, heading to the rear of the store to get her phone. "I'll ask if he knows anything."

"No need." Nicole noticed a man entering the shop. "Here he is now."

Claire turned and her heart skipped a beat when she saw Ian near the door. Dressed in a dark, fitted suit, the detective moved like an athlete as he approached the girls. "Have you heard?"

Claire nodded and when several customers came in, she, Ian, and Nicole moved to the work room and Robby went out front to handle the orders.

"Robby gets news alerts on his phone," Claire said. "He just told us."

Ian kept his voice low. His dark brown eyes were filled with concern. "I think it would be best if you two stop interviewing people about Grace Dodd's death."

"You think it's dangerous?" Nicole wrapped her arms around herself.

"I don't know, but better to be safe than sorry. We don't know what we're dealing with yet. The deaths of Mrs. Dodd and Representative Lowe could be coincidence. Until we know more, I'd feel better if you stay clear of it."

"How did she die?" Claire asked. "Are you able to say?"

Ian hesitated. "I'll just say it wasn't from natural causes."

Nicole let out a gasp as Claire's stomach lurched.

"What's going on?" Nicole whispered. "Did someone kill her and Grace Dodd?" She sank onto a chair.

Claire held Ian's eyes. "Do you think Vanessa or Maddy could be in danger?"

"The investigation has only started. We don't know much. If we find out there's a link between the deaths, then we'll make a determination if anyone else might be at risk." Ian's phone buzzed in his pocket and he removed it to read the message. "I need to go." He looked from Claire to Nicole. "Keep a low profile for a while, okay? Stay safe."

When Ian left the room, Nicole looked up at her friend, worry etched over her face. "Could you talk to Tessa? I have a feeling we're going to need your skills in top form very soon."

Anxiety flashed through Claire's body. The mess was getting bigger.

11

————

Claire collected the Corgis from Tony's market, took them for a long walk, and as the sun headed for the horizon, she returned home to her apartment to cook dinner. The condo apartment was located in a brick townhouse at the edge of Beacon Hill in a small neighborhood of historic brownstone townhouses known as Adamsburg Square. The neighborhood had several cobblestone streets, brick walkways, and old-fashioned streetlamps. Claire's place had a large living room with three enormous windows and a sliding glass door that opened to a small garden with a bit of grass, two shade trees, and a patio all enclosed by a high white fence. There was a large dining room, a beautiful kitchen, a small private basement, and two bedrooms.

Sitting on the small brick patio under the branches of the big tree, she and Nicole ate home-made pizza and green salad as the dogs rested near the fence that separated the townhouse's outside space from the building next to Claire's.

"Did you get that loose picket in the fence fixed yet?" Nicole cut a piece from her pizza slice.

"No," Claire laughed. "Having the unattached picket worked out well for me last month. I'm thinking of leaving it the way it is." In the middle of another mystery, Claire was attacked in her home and the Corgis pushed through the fence and ran to Tony's to alert him to the trouble. Tony made calls that sent the police to the townhouse just in time to help Claire.

"Probably a good idea," Nicole agreed.

After finishing the food, Claire brought her laptop out to the patio table. "Let's look up the train schedules from Boston to Greendale to see what time Maddy would have arrived at home." Tapping at the keyboard brought up the subway and commuter rail times. "Here it is. We left the Opera House around what time do you think?"

Nicole calculated. "The show finished, we met

Vanessa and Maddy in the lobby and talked. They both had to leave to catch the trains, so I'd estimate we all left around 10:30pm."

"Okay." Claire scanned the time schedule. "Maddy would have caught the 10:50 train and arrived at the Greendale station around 11:20."

"Walking to her house from the station would only take about five minutes," Nicole said. "Vanessa called us around midnight so the timeframe works."

"If she took a cab," Claire surmised, "then Maddy probably would have arrived at the house around 11pm. Plenty of time to argue with her mother."

"I don't see how we'd be able to figure out whether or not she took a cab. Maybe the police can get information about fares to Greendale that night." Nicole nodded at the laptop. "Look up the trains to New York. I hate doing this. I feel like a spy, like I don't trust a friend."

Claire brought up the next schedule. "You really don't know Vanessa that well. It's been years since you hung out with her in high school. People can change. We have to consider every angle."

Scanning the time schedule, Nicole pointed. "The last train is at 9:30pm."

Claire looked at her friend. "We were in the concert hall at 9:30."

"Oh, no." Nicole's face paled.

"Did we mishear?" Claire tapped at the keyboard. "Maybe she took a bus." Checking the schedules of five different bus companies, the two sat staring at the screen in silence.

"No bus departs the city for New York around the time Vanessa said she was leaving." Nicole's shoulders sagged.

Claire's neck muscles tightened with tension. "We need to ask her about this."

"How can we bring it up? This is terrible. Did she go home, fight with her mother, and then take off to make it seem like she was returning from the train? It would explain her father's weird behavior. He could have heard the argument. He might be trying to protect Vanessa." Nicole placed her hands on her stomach. "I feel sick."

"Vanessa might be the person Maddy saw from the window." Claire rubbed her temple and a wave of dizziness washed over her. "But, maybe not."

"Why are you saying that?" Nicole sounded hopeful.

"I get the impression Vanessa wasn't there when her mother fell."

"An impression? Like a *special* impression or a normal person's impression?"

With a frown, Claire cocked her head. "I *am* a normal person."

"That's debatable." Nicole smiled. "Which is it? Is it an impression that other people might pick up on or not?"

"I don't know." Claire gave a shrug, and then brightened. "But Vanessa's story *must* work out. The police had to have checked on it. It must be okay. Let's talk to her."

Nicole agreed, but told Claire that she would have to be the one that brought it up. "Look up Representative Lowe. See if there's any news about her death."

Claire did an internet search and several articles came up. "Here's the most recent one." Scanning the new story, she said, "State Representative Victoria Lowe, age 53, was found dead in her Beacon Hill townhouse this afternoon. Preliminary reports indicate that Ms. Lowe was discovered at the bottom of the staircase leading to the basement. An anonymous source reported that Ms. Lowe had apparently broken her neck from a fall down the stairs. A laundry basket was found next to the body."

Nicole grimaced. "How awful. She must have fallen on her way down to the laundry room."

Claire narrowed her eyes. "Or she was pushed."

"Oh." The word came out of Nicole's throat like a moan. "Someone might have placed the basket next to her to make it look like an accident."

"I wonder where Dr. Dodd was when Ms. Lowe took a tumble."

Nicole made a face. "Two dead women and they both had a relationship with that man."

"Suspicious, isn't it?" Claire leaned back from the laptop. Shadows gathered in the yard and the little white twinkling lights strung between the tree's branches sparkled on.

"Why would he kill both of them? I can see him having a fight with Grace over his affair, but why on earth would he then kill his lover?" Nicole slid the laptop closer. "Does it say who found the body at the bottom of the stairs?"

A warm breeze fluttered the leaves while the girls read through the article.

"It doesn't say." Claire noticed the Corgis sitting at attention and a ripple of worry slipped over her skin.

"Maybe Ian can tell us."

Nicole's phone buzzed with a text. "It's from

Vanessa. She wants to meet. She's not far from the chocolate shop. What should I say? You want to meet her?"

"Sure. Ask her if she's okay."

Nicole pressed on her phone screen. "I sent it."

In a few seconds, a new message arrived, and Nicole lifted her eyes after reading it. "She says she'd rather talk in person."

"Okay." Claire stood to clear the table. "Let's go, but I want to take the dogs along and I'd like to take a detour."

LEADING the way into the Beacon Hill neighborhood, Claire found Victoria Lowe's townhouse and the foursome slowed as they approached the building. A few young gawkers stood across the street under a lamplight staring at the house. The dogs whined as they got closer to the house.

"How do Bear and Lady know something bad happened here?" Nicole asked softly.

"Maybe they smell it." Claire had no idea how the Corgis seemed to know and sense things.

Nicole elbowed her friend with a grin. "Is that how you know stuff? You sniff it?"

Stopping next to the four people looking at the townhouse, Claire ignored Nicole's joke and asked them, "Are the police inside?"

A tall, skinny young man replied. "Not anymore. They were here for a long time earlier in the evening. They all left."

"Does it seem like anyone else lives there?"

"No one's gone in or out except the police so maybe not."

Claire touched Nicole's arm. "Let's walk around to the back."

They found the small alleyway that ran behind the townhouse and headed up the cobblestone walkway.

"What are you planning?" Nicole asked with a tinge of worry in her voice.

"Nothing. I just want to get closer to the building without prying eyes watching us." Standing directly behind the brick structure, Claire squatted down near the small basement windows and, placing her palm against the glass, she closed her eyes.

Both Corgis whined and fidgeted.

Taking slow breaths in and out, Claire tried to open her mind to anything floating on the air. She could feel her muscles relaxing and she stayed in the position for nearly five minutes. As she was about to give up, a bright white light flashed in her head and a sensation like something hitting her in the chest sent her sprawling on her butt. Bear and Lady jumped and rushed to their owner, sniffing and nervously darting around her.

"I'm okay," Claire reassured the animals.

Nicole knelt beside her friend. "What was that? What happened?"

Rubbing her forehead, Claire stayed sitting. "I don't know what it was." She described what she'd felt and Nicole's eyes widened.

"You felt like you were struck on the chest?" Nicole stared at the basement window and crawled closer to get a look inside. With her face pressed up against the glass, she said, "I can't see anything in there. The basement's too dark." She turned back to Claire. "You must have sensed Ms. Lowe getting punched in the chest. The blow must have sent her falling down the stairs. That must be what you felt."

"That could be." Claire's head felt groggy. "But I wonder, though ... I wonder if she could have had a heart attack when she was walking down the stairs. I feel something odd about the heart."

"A heart attack? I wasn't expecting that." Nicole sat on the gravelly cement next to Claire. "Well, maybe there was no foul play involved at all. Maybe her death was from natural causes."

Claire put her hand against her chest and could feel her heart beat falling back into its normal rhythm.

A sudden gust of wind blew small particles of dirt and gravel from the alley into the girls' faces causing Nicole to groan. "Let's get out of here. Are you okay? Are you able to stand up? Sitting here in the dark is giving me the creeps. I hope Victoria Lowe hasn't turned into a ghost."

Claire chuckled as the young women stood and brushed dirt from their backsides. "If she's a ghost now, maybe she can help us out by telling us what happened to her. Why don't we stick around and see if she shows up?" she kidded.

"No way." Nicole hurried ahead following the Corgis out of the alleyway muttering about how she wished they'd brought a flashlight. "You can stay if you want."

When Claire looked back at the basement window for a moment, the little hairs on her arms stood up and a cold shiver ran down her back.

What really happened in there?

12

V anessa was standing in front of the chocolate shop when Nicole, Claire, and the Corgis showed up to meet with her. The dogs wiggled their tails when they were introduced and Vanessa gave each one some cheek scratches. "What nice dogs," she smiled.

Upstairs in Nicole's apartment, everyone settled on the sofas while the Corgis inspected the place sniffing around the four rooms. Vanessa's face looked tired and drawn and the rims of her eyes were red. "Thanks for meeting me. You must have heard the news about my father's 'friend'?" She made air quotation marks with her hands when she said the word *friend*. When I was at work, Maddy texted me to say Dad left a note on the kitchen table that he'd gone away for a few days." Vanessa rolled her eyes. "Really? If he's not guilty, he'll make everyone think he is by his behavior."

"When did he leave?" Nicole asked.

"This afternoon." Vanessa shook her head. "Why would he take off? It's the stupidest thing he could have done. Has he lost his mind? The police will want to talk to him."

"Where did he go?" Claire still felt light-headed from her experience behind Victoria Lowe's townhouse.

"We have a house in Marblehead. I bet he went there."

"Should you call him?" Nicole asked. "See how he is? Encourage him to come home?"

"I don't know what to do." Vanessa sank back against the sofa's throw pillows and when tears started down her cheeks, she leaned forward and buried her face in her hands.

Nicole ran for a box of tissues and put her arm around her friend's shoulders. After a few minutes, Vanessa raised her head and dabbed at her cheeks. "I feel like I've been run over by a bus. My mom's dead and I'm afraid my father caused her death. It's as if I'm a supporting actor in some terrible, awful movie. I've always felt safe, secure, loved. Now I'm free-falling out of the sky waiting to hit the ground. My family, God ... what a terrible reversal of fortune."

Claire understood the sensation of falling, falling into the pit of grief from losing a loved one ... her own mother, Teddy. The world shifted beneath your feet while you grasped for something to hold onto and you were never the same person you were before the loss. Gripping her hands together tightly, she wanted to say something comforting to Vanessa, but anything she thought of seemed so pathetically inadequate.

"You'll get through it," Nicole said softly as she rubbed the woman's back.

"I have to be strong for Maddy." Vanessa brushed the wetness from her face. "I want to understand what's going on. Thank you for helping, for talking to people for me."

Nicole and Claire exchanged a quick look. "Um," Nicole started. "A detective told us that we shouldn't talk to anyone else."

Vanessa's eyes went wide. "Who? Why? The police can't stop you from talking to anyone."

"I think it's more a concern for safety," Claire told her. "Until they can figure out if the same person is responsible for both deaths."

The three sat without saying anything for a few minutes until Claire brought up the question she and Nicole had been worrying over. "You know when you told us you were on the train to New York the night of the accident, did you misspeak? Did you mean you were on the bus?" Claire knew very well that there wasn't a bus heading to New York that late either, but she thought it was a gentler way of broaching the topic than coming right out and accusing Vanessa of lying.

A slight look of panic flashed over Vanessa's face and she swallowed hard. "What do you mean?"

"I don't think there's a late train to New York." Claire's impulse was to squirm in her seat, but she managed to stay still. "I needed to get to New York not too long ago and there wasn't a train that ran so late." Now Claire was the one who was lying and it made her feel uncomfortable.

"I ... I...." Vanessa stammered and then batted at the air. "I lied about it. The police caught me in it, too. I'm not very good with coming up with a story."

Relief washed over Claire's and Nicole's faces, both glad that Vanessa was going to come clean.

"I wasn't on my way to New York." Vanessa let out a long sigh. "I've recently started seeing someone and I was heading to Cape Cod to meet him. I was planning to stay with a friend for a couple of days and then meet this guy on his boat. He had a business meeting on the Cape the day after tomorrow, then we were going to meet, spend time on the boat, go to the beach, have dinner. I rented a car. When I got Maddy's call, I turned the car around and dropped it off in the city so I could grab a cab home."

Listening to Vanessa talk, a shiver of unease ran over Claire's skin.

"Why so secretive about going to the Cape?" Nicole asked.

"Maddy met him once. She doesn't like him."

Something itched at Claire. "Why not?"

"She said she thinks he's full of himself, selfish, only cares about himself." Vanessa shook her head. "She met him for about thirty minutes one time. I don't know how she could get that idea in such a short amount of time."

Claire thought it was certainly possible to get an idea of someone in that amount of time, but she decided not to voice that opinion.

"So I made up the story about needing to go to New York for three days for work. I know it's rotten, but I'd like to get to know this guy and I didn't want Maddy upset with me."

"Where did you meet him?" Nicole asked.

"In a coffee shop," Vanessa replied. "It was crowded and he sat at my table."

"Did your parents meet him?" Claire asked.

"No. I told my mom I'd been on some dates with someone, but it's too new. First, I have to decide if I like him and see if he likes me."

"What does he do?" Nicole questioned.

"He's a developer. He owns some strip malls, a few hotels."

"How did he behave towards Maddy when they met?"

"He was cordial. He's older. I don't think he knows how to interact with a teenager. I think he and Maddy would be fine once they got to know each other better." Vanessa pushed her hair back over her shoulder and gave a shrug. "Maddy can get jealous. She really hasn't liked any of my boyfriends."

"Have the police called you about your father?" Claire asked.

"Not yet. They have his cell number. Maybe they've already talked to him. I just think running off right after that woman was found dead makes him look really bad." Vanessa balled her hands into fists. "Could he have killed my mother and that woman? I wish he'd talk to me. I don't know what to do."

"Does he have a close friend he might be able to talk with?" Claire suggested.

"He has a close friend at the hospital, another doctor. I don't know if he'd confide in him."

"I wonder if you should call the friend," Nicole said. "Ask if you could meet. Tell him you're worried about your father."

Claire nodded. "Maybe between the two of you, you could convince your father to get some counseling. He might need an outlet to talk with someone that doesn't involve family or friends. Your father might feel that discussing his feelings would only serve to upset everyone more, so he stays quiet and bottles things up."

"I don't know," Vanessa muttered. "Maybe."

To brighten the mood if only for a little while, Nicole suggested tea and pieces of chocolate mousse cake and they moved to the small round dining table near the window to enjoy the evening snack. The Corgis each got two dog treats and they happily munched on them before settling in the corner while the humans' chat turned to lighter subjects.

Vanessa's phone buzzed and she read the text. "It's the guy I've been seeing. He's asked me to meet for a drink. I'm going to go."

Nicole nodded. "I think it will be good to take your mind off things for a little while."

Vanessa gave her friends a hug, patted the dogs, and left the apartment to meet the man in the Back Bay.

"I'm so glad that's been cleared up." Nicole took some of the dishes to the kitchen and Claire followed with the cake platter and some tea cups. "I'm so relieved there was a reason she told the fib."

"Yeah," Claire said.

Nicole turned around and gave Claire the eye. "You look a million miles away."

Giving herself a shake, Claire smiled. "Thinking everything over, that's all."

"Is something bothering you?"

"The whole mess bothers me."

Nicole said. "I mean something specific. You look like you're giving something a lot of thought."

Claire loaded the dishwasher. "When Vanessa talked about her new guy and spoke about Maddy, I got a funny feeling."

Nicole's lips pulled down at the corners. "How do you mean a funny feeling?"

"I don't know." Claire held a plate over the dish-washer rack for a few seconds before loading it while she thought about what was picking at her.

Nicole stepped closer. "Where in the conversation did you start to get the sensation?"

"It started up when Vanessa was telling us why she made up the lie. It was an odd feeling of anxiety." Claire looked off into space. "It got stronger when...."

"When what?"

"When Vanessa mentioned that Maddy could be jealous...." Claire looked at her friend. "I don't know why, but something about what Vanessa told us made me feel ... nervous."

13

Nicole borrowed a friend's car and drove Claire and the Corgis to Greendale so they could walk around Vanessa's family's neighborhood and take a look in the rear yard of the home where Maddy claimed to have seen someone step into the woods on the night Grace Dodd fell from the window. Vanessa was at work, but she said her father was still in Marblehead and Maddy went to MIT to talk with a professor so the house was empty and no one would be around while they investigated.

Nicole pulled the car to a stop on a side street and she and her passengers got out. The branches of the mature trees hung over the road creating a green leaf canopy above the sidewalks and the street.

"I hope nobody calls the police and has the car towed." Nicole locked the doors.

"Your friend will really appreciate it if you get his car towed to a lot somewhere," Claire kidded. "I think it will be okay. There's a park up ahead. I bet people leave their cars here sometimes so they can go to the park." Glancing around, she asked, "Which way is the Dodd's street?"

"That way." Nicole pointed. "I'm not sure if the park goes up behind their house or not. After I left town, a parcel of land was donated to expand the park, but I'm not sure how far it goes."

"Shall we walk through the park and see where it goes or should we go directly to the Dodd's house first?" Claire asked.

"Let's go to the house. Then we can walk in the yard and see what's behind it." Nicole led the way down the quiet, side street to another road that would lead them to the Dodds.

"It's such a pretty neighborhood." Claire admired the large, well-tended homes lining both sides of the street. "It must have been a nice place to grow up ... and so close to the city, too."

Nicole agreed and told Claire about some adventures she and her friends had in high school. "We got into trouble more than a few times. It was never anything serious, just silly teenage hijinks. We had fun." Approaching the handsome Victorian belonging to the Dodds, Nicole said, "Here we are."

They stood on the sidewalk looking over the house and gardens while the Corgis sniffed along the wrought-iron fence.

"It's sure a pretty place." Claire admired the vivid green lawn, the flowers blooming in the manicured beds, and the large porch sweeping around the front and side of the house. "No one would ever suspect the sadness and turmoil going on inside."

Nicole and Claire moved into the yard with the dogs and headed for the spot under the third floor window. A bit of broken glass still remained mixed in with the blades of grass. Staring up to the top floor, Nicole let out a sigh. "It's hard for me to believe that Mrs. Dodd fell out of that window. What the heck happened up there?"

Claire kept her eyes on the window. "Vanessa said the police told her there was no sign of forced entry or any indication of an intruder, but that doesn't mean there wasn't one."

"Wouldn't Dr. Dodd have heard an intruder? Especially if whoever broke in chased his wife up to the third floor. She would have been screaming, wouldn't she?"

"I'd think so," Claire agreed. "Unless the intruder threatened to hurt Dr. Dodd if Grace didn't do what he told her to do."

"God." Nicole's shoulders slumped as she turned away from the house. "I can't look at that window for another second. My heart starts racing from imagining Grace falling from the third floor." Facing the tree line, she asked, "Do you want to stay near the house a little longer?"

"I think so." Claire thought she should stand below the window for a short while. "I'll see if I can sense anything. I won't need much time."

"I'll walk the dogs around the backyard while you're busy. Come get us when you're ready." Nicole headed for the rear of the property with Bear and Lady bouncing along beside her eager to sniff and investigate the new place.

Claire sank onto the grass and noticed a small piece of fractured glass next to her. She reached over and carefully touched it with her index finger, then closed her eyes and tried to chase any thoughts from her mind. After only a minute, quick flashes of images jumped in her brain.

Rushing up the stairs. The blood mark on the wood-work of the third floor bedroom threshold. Dr. Dodd in his office. A person being struck by someone else. A scream and the shatter of glass. The shadow of someone standing near the dark trees. A sense of plummeting like when you're just about to sleep and you startle awake from the feeling of falling. Claire's eyelids flew open as she jerked to alertness.

Beads of sweat trickled down her back and her heart pounded with such force she thought it would burst through her chest wall. Pushing up from the lawn, Claire shook herself and went to find Nicole and the Corgis.

"Were they images from what actually happened or from imagining what happened?" Nicole asked after Claire reported what she'd experienced.

"I don't really know." Claire's long, blond curls bounced as she shook her head. "I've got a headache from it."

"Shall we go home?"

"No, let's see what's beyond the trees."

The dogs led the way and bounded between the trees into the wooded area while Claire and Nicole stopped and looked back to the house.

"I think Maddy was right." Claire rubbed at her temple. "Someone was here that night."

Nicole eyed her friend. "Do you get a feeling of who it might be?"

"No." Claire gave a weary smile. "Wouldn't it be helpful if I did?"

"Yup," Nicole kidded. "You need to hone your skills."

The dogs barked from a few yards into the trees and the girls hurried to see what caught their attention.

"It's part of the park." Nicole pointed. "Look. There's a walking path here. It must lead back to the park."

With one hand on her hip, Claire turned in a circle glancing up and down the trail that ran behind the houses situated along the Dodd's street. "Well, this is convenient, isn't it? Park where we did, walk up the path, sneak into the Dodd's backyard, and enter the house. Kill Grace and then escape into the woods."

"If that's what happened, then it would mean that Dr. Dodd didn't kill his wife."

Claire made eye contact with her friend. "Or, someone was out walking that night. They heard the commotion at the house, stepped into the Dodd's yard, saw Grace fall, maybe got a look at the killer, got scared, and rushed away."

"A witness." Nicole nodded. "It makes sense."

"The police must have checked this out," Claire

said. "They must be thinking the same thing we are. I bet they've talked to the neighbors, asked if anyone was out walking that night. Maybe someone gave them some good information."

Nicole crossed her arms over her chest. "And I bet they didn't find out anything important."

"Why do you say that?" Claire tilted her head.

"Because the District Attorney's office would have told Vanessa if there was a good clue or something helpful," Nicole noted. "I bet nobody knows anything. It's been days since Grace died. This mess isn't going to be solved anytime soon."

"Is that what *your* intuition tells you?" One side of Claire's mouth went up.

Nicole winked. "Maybe *my* intuition is getting stronger from hanging around with you."

Claire bent to scratch the dogs' ears. "I think we all make a good team."

Bear and Lady woofed in agreement.

"Shall we walk back to the car along the path?" Nicole asked.

"Sure," Claire nodded and as she was about to follow along the trail, some movement near the Dodd's house caught her and Lady's eyes. "Nic," she spoke softly. "There's someone at the house."

Nicole hurried to Claire's side and peered

between the branches. "A woman. Maybe it's the housekeeper."

"Good idea. Shall we go introduce ourselves?"

"You bet."

"If it *is* the housekeeper and since no one is at home," Claire suggested, "she might be more willing to speak freely. We might get some helpful tidbits from her."

Nicole and the dogs pushed through the trees. "Or she'll call the police on us for trespassing."

"One way to find out."

The Corgis and the young women walked across the lawn towards the woman who stood with her hands on hips staring at the group as they approached. And she wasn't smiling.

14

Nicole waved at the petite, stocky, gray-haired woman who looked increasingly alarmed the closer Claire, Nicole, and the dogs got to her. "We're friends of Vanessa. We were walking on the path from the park."

The woman eyed them warily, and although she seemed to be relaxing slightly, she had an expression that said she wanted these intruders to go away. "Vanessa isn't home." Despite her short stature, the woman's arms were toned and her body appeared strong with a contained energy embedded in her muscles.

"Are you a family friend?" Claire asked with a smile.

The woman snorted and her light blue eyes flashed. "I'm the housekeeper."

"Do you take care of the yard, too?" Claire wondered why the housekeeper was outside the house.

With a vigorous shake of the head, the woman said, "I saw you from the window. I wondered why you were prowling around, staring at the house."

Nicole asked, "How long have you worked for the Dodds?"

"A long time," the woman's voice held a grumpy tone.

"I've known Vanessa since we were in school together here in Greendale. Did you start working for the Dodds right after Vanessa went to college?"

"Ten years." The woman nodded and kicked her toe in the grass.

Nicole stretched out her hand to shake. "I'm Nicole Summers and this is my friend, Claire Rollins."

The woman gave Nicole's hand a look of displeasure, but took hold of it anyway. "Edie Brookhaven."

"We're sorry about Mrs. Dodd," Claire told Edie.

Edie glanced down at the ground. "Yeah."

"Did you work that day?" Claire kept her voice even. "Did you notice anything that seemed off?"

"Off? How?" Edie took a quick look at Claire and then shifted her eyes downward.

"Did it seem like a regular day? Did the Dodds act like anything was wrong?"

Edie had on a full apron that tied behind her waist and neck. She shoved her hands into the wide front pocket. "Same as always, far as I could tell."

"Are you usually here every day?" Nicole asked.

"Usually five days a week. Eight to five."

"You probably don't see much of Dr. Dodd since he must be at work when you're here," Claire observed. She couldn't help but think that something was simmering under the surface of this woman.

"Sometimes he works from home. I make his meals when he's at home. I usually make the family's evening meal before I leave for the day."

"How are they to work for?" Claire watched Edie's face and saw a flicker wash over her for a moment.

"Fine."

"Was Mrs. Dodd at home on the day she died?" Nicole took a look up to the third floor window and quickly turned her eyes away.

"She was here." Edie shook her head. "You never know what the future holds, I guess. Here today, gone tomorrow." Deep wrinkles ran over the woman's forehead and along the sides of her mouth. She had a missing tooth and some other teeth were crooked in the gum. Edie gave the impression of a life hard-lived and Claire couldn't figure out if it was a result of hard work and low wages or if substance-abuse might have played a role in aging the woman.

"Did you like Mrs. Dodd?" Nicole asked.

"She was fine."

"How about Dr. Dodd? Did you like him?"

"I didn't have much to do with the doctor." A gruffness seemed to color the sentence. "I did my work, that was it."

"And Maddy? You worked here from when she was about ten years old?" Claire asked.

Edie's eyes brightened. "Yup. Maddy's an angel. A sweet girl. Smart, too."

"Do you live in Greendale?" Claire questioned.

Edie gave a look of disbelief that anyone would ask such a question. "Me? In Greendale? No, I do not. I live in Dorchester."

"Do you ever stay late at the Dodds to work?"

Making eye contact briefly with Claire, Edie rubbed her arm with her hand. "Once in a while. Why all these questions?"

Nicole took in a deep breath and decided to give

their inquiry an air of authority to see if they could get more information from the housekeeper. "Vanessa has hired Claire to look into Mrs. Dodd's death. Claire is an attorney."

"Oh." Edie gave Claire a long look. "You find out anything yet?"

"I've been gathering information, interviewing people." Claire nodded. "I'm piecing things together right now."

Edie blinked at Claire assessing this news. "Do you want to go sit on the porch and get out of the hot sun?"

The group moved to the front porch and the Corgis followed after the three people as they made their way to the rocking chairs to sit while they talked. The dogs sat down in the shade of the covered porch. Edie gave the animals a long look. "Who do the dogs belong to?"

Bear and Lady moved closer to the woman and wagged their little tails.

"They're mine," Claire said. "They're good dogs. They helped save me from an attack once."

"Did they?" Edie's face softened as she reached to pat the friendly Corgis. "I always liked dogs."

"Do you have one?"

"No. Too hard to have a dog in an apartment.

Maybe someday, if I ever live on the first floor. I'd like a dog of my own."

Claire waited a few moments before asking, "Did Mrs. Dodd seem her usual self the day she died?"

"Yeah, she did, if by usual, you mean, was she angry."

"Was she angry a lot?"

"Recently, you might say."

Nicole nodded. "Vanessa told us about Dr. Dodd's affair."

Edie's lips tightened. "Did she tell you her father accused her mother of having an affair?"

Claire's eyes widened. "Mrs. Dodd was having an affair?"

Edie scoffed. "No, she was not. Maybe the doctor accused her to make his own affair seem legit. You know, blame the wife … and pretend he was having an affair only because she was having one."

"Did you hear this or did Mrs. Dodd tell you?"

A sigh slipped from Edie's throat. "I was here late one night, baking for an event the Dodds were having on the weekend. I heard them arguing in his office." A cloud settled over her face and Edie bit her lower lip. "Dr. Dodd said he wouldn't have started his affair if Grace hadn't been having one. Grace flew into a rage. She called him names, called him a miserable liar. She said he made the whole thing up to justify his own fling."

"What did Dr. Dodd say to that?"

"I went into the hall to hear better. I got scared. I heard him tell Grace that he'd gone through her phone records trying to find the person she was meeting up with. Grace threw something across the room, that's what I thought anyway. The door was closed. Something shattered. She screamed at him. She told him never to invade her privacy again. She called him an old whore, told him he was sickening, and to never accuse her of his own disgusting infidelity." Edie looked down at the emerald lawn stretching out to the sidewalk. "I heard what sounded like punches. The doctor yelled at her to stop. I guess Grace was hitting him. I think he hit her, too. I moved back towards the kitchen. I didn't want them to find me standing there if they came out of the office."

Claire asked, "When did this happen?"

Edie's face was solemn. "The night before Grace died."

"What happened next? Did Grace and Dr. Dodd keep fighting?" Nicole's eyes were wide.

"Grace came out of the office and I rushed into the kitchen to pretend I didn't hear anything that was going on. Grace came into the kitchen to get a dishtowel. Her hand was cut and she wrapped it up with the towel. I offered to help. She sat in one of the kitchen chairs. She told me to go home. I asked if she was okay. She told me *yes, go ahead home now*. I told her I'd finish up the baking and head home."

"Did things stay quiet then?"

"Grace went upstairs. I waited for the cake to finish baking and then I cleaned up. Dr. Dodd came into the kitchen. He looked surprised to see me there. He turned around and walked out without saying anything. There was blood on his temple." Edie pointed to the side of her face to indicate where the man's wound was. "I hate to say it, but I was secretly glad he had an injury, too. He was the one who caused the trouble. It's all his fault." Some beads of sweat showed on the woman's forehead and her face flushed red. "It's all his fault," she muttered.

Claire asked carefully, "Do you mean it's Dr. Dodd's fault that Grace fell?"

Edie's voice was almost a whisper. "It's his fault Grace is dead."

Leaning towards Edie, Claire chose her words with care and spoke softly. "Do you think Dr. Dodd is responsible for Grace's fall?"

Edie blinked and straightened. "What?" She

brushed at the sweat on her brow, stood abruptly, and hurried to the front door of the house. "Sorry. I have to get back to work. You can sit here as long as you want." With a click, the door closed after her.

The Corgis jumped up and whined.

Nicole stared at the shiny black door of the house. "Why the sudden end to the conversation?"

"Did I ask a question that was too difficult to answer?" A cold, hard hand of anxiety gripped Claire's stomach.

15

Claire sat on a small stool stocking the lower shelves in the store room of Tony's market. Since sitting with the housekeeper on the porch the previous day, Claire had been puzzling over the things Edie had told her and Nicole. More than once, the woman said that Grace's death was Dr. Dodd's fault. What exactly did she mean? Was Dr. Dodd at fault indirectly because of his affair and the impact it had on the marriage or was he the direct cause, did he push Grace from the window? Finishing her task and heading to ask Tony what else she could do to help him, questions swirled in Claire's head and she wanted to talk to Edie again about the Dodds and what else might have happened between them.

When she stepped out of the store room, Claire spotted Tony talking to a customer who was hidden from view by a tall shelf. Claire couldn't remember seeing the man look so bright-eyed and energetic and she wondered who he was talking to. Bear and Lady sat next to Tony wagging their tails.

Tony spotted Claire hesitating in the aisle. "Your friend's here." His voice practically sparkled and when Claire moved forward, she saw Tessa, the clairvoyant she'd met last month, standing in front of Tony. The woman turned to Claire and wrapped her in a hug.

"I got out of work ahead of schedule so I'm early. Hope that's okay." Tessa worked a few blocks from the small market and deli, so she and Claire decided to meet there when Tessa was ready.

"I've been helping Tony while I waited for you. I see you've met." With a raised eyebrow and a sly smile, Claire looked over Tessa's shoulder and caught Tony's eye. The big man's cheeks were flushed pink and his eyes were shining. He shifted his gaze back to Tessa to avoid Claire's scrutiny.

"Do you have a bathroom I can use before we leave?" Tessa asked and Tony pointed out the way to the tiny restroom tucked in a back corner.

"So," Claire started in on her friend once Tessa was gone. "I saw you making moon eyes at Tessa."

"What? You're imagining things, Blondie." Tony scurried behind the counter and pretended to arrange things. "I'm being friendly is all. I'm welcoming your friend."

"Yes, right." Claire sidled up to the counter with a grin. "Is that why you're blushing?"

Tony turned away to fiddle with something on the far counter. "I was out in the sun," he muttered.

"I see." Claire couldn't suppress a chuckle. Hearing the restroom door open, she leaned over the counter and whispered, "Tessa isn't married by the way."

Tony growled low in his throat, but his face lit up when he saw auburn-haired Tessa coming towards them.

"All set," Tessa said. "Shall we go?"

Claire put leashes on the dogs. Tessa took hold of one, smiled at Tony and told him how nice it was to meet him, and headed for the door.

Giving the man a hug, Claire said softly, "I'll put in a good word with her for you." Tony scowled at Claire as she left the market with a wide grin over her face.

With the sun low in the sky, the women walked

up the brick sidewalks to Beacon Hill, all the while, Claire giving a monologue about the latest twists in the Grace Dodd case and asking Tessa a million questions about paranormal skills.

Tessa tossed her head back and laughed. "I'm no expert you know. There isn't a manual that explains it all. I can only advise you based on my own experiences and the experiences of those who've confided in me. A lot of what you're asking I don't have an answer for."

Claire frowned. "It's all just too complicated."

"You have to live with your skills for a while, become accustomed to them, learn what you can do and what you can't do."

"Last month, I felt things strongly and my feelings were correct. Now, I'm only getting little hints of sensations and I don't know if they're simply the intuition that a normal person would feel or if I'm actually sensing something more ... more, what? Paranormal? Is that the word I should use?"

Tessa said, "You can use any word that suits."

"Am I losing the skill that started to show up last month? Could it be disappearing?" Claire's lips turned down.

"Don't push." Tessa waited for Bear to sniff around the bottom of a light post. "If you try too hard and get stressed over it then you might not sense anything. It's a subtle skill that you have. You need to be open-minded and clear-headed so that unseen information that floats through the world is available to you."

"That makes sense." Claire nodded. "I'm impatient though. I want to be able to help, but I get wound up and anxious, and a lot of the time, I don't sense anything at all."

"You're learning about your ability. Give it time and practice, but remember, you can't force this and the harder you push at it, the more it will float away from you."

"What if I'm losing my skill?" Claire's voice was tinged with hopelessness. "Last month when this started, I didn't want this darned skill and now I'm afraid it's going away."

"Time will tell." Tessa puffed. "This hill is killing me."

"We're almost there. Do you want to stop to catch your breath?"

"I'm okay. I just need to get in shape."

"You can train each day with me and Ian, if you like," Claire offered.

Tessa rolled her eyes. "I'll leave that nonsense to you two. I was thinking of just getting out and walking more." A bead of sweat trickled down the woman's temple. "Tony seems very nice."

With a little smile creeping over her face, Claire gave Tessa a sideways look. "He's super nice. A good guy, the best. He's like a dad to me. I love Tony."

"Does he have family?"

Claire stopped and turned to Tessa. "If you mean, is he married, the answer is no, he's not. He's single."

"Oh, no," Tessa blustered. "I didn't mean that. I was only asking about him in general."

"Hmm." A smile plastered over Claire's mouth. "I saw the way you two were ogling each other."

"What? No we weren't."

Claire could see a flush of pink coloring Tessa's cheeks. "I didn't need any paranormal abilities to see it. It would have been plain as day to anyone who happened to be in the store."

Lady woofed and wiggled her tail.

"Don't you start in on me, too," Tessa kidded with the dog.

"Here we are." Claire nodded to the small cobblestone street. "This is where State Representative Lowe lived. Two townhouses up from here."

Tessa eyed the road and the surroundings. "Let's walk past the house."

Shadows from the setting sun spread over the old, bumpy lane and a little chill surrounded them from the breeze changing direction over the ocean.

"It's this one on the left." Claire indicated the house.

Tessa took a look at the three-story brick structure and then turned her eyes to the street corner a few houses up the road where the figure of a man stood leaning against the streetlight post. When he saw the women, he started to walk towards them, moving with a slight limp and leaning on the cane he held in his right hand. Dressed in black slacks, a black v-neck sweater, a black suit jacket, and a black fedora hat, the man's silver-gray hair touched the top of his collar.

Claire stiffened and the dogs, on alert to the approaching person, kept their eyes locked on the man. Sensing their worry, Tessa said, "I know him. It's okay. I asked him to meet us here."

The man gave a nod and Tessa made introductions. When he took Claire's hand to shake, electricity zipped up her arm and she almost pulled back.

"Maxwell, this is Claire. As I told you, she shares similar intuitive skills."

"Hello, Claire." The man's voice was deep and almost soothing.

"I've known Maxwell for years. Let's all walk around to the alleyway that runs behind the building."

As Claire led the way to the cobblestone alley, Tessa turned her ankle on the uneven surface and let out a curse. "I know these roads are charming, but they're killing me. I never get used to walking on them."

Maxwell offered his arm and the woman took hold of it.

Claire and the Corgis stopped at the back of Victoria Lowe's townhouse. "This is it."

Tessa leaned to Claire. "I haven't told Maxwell anything about what happened here. I asked for him to come and give his opinion."

Claire wasn't exactly sure what that meant, but she gave a nod.

Maxwell took his time looking up and down the brick building until his eyes settled on the basement window. He moved forward and stared at the glass. He placed his hand against the side of the town-house and lifted his cane until the end tip touched the basement window glass. He held it there for a long time.

Bear looked up at Claire and whined.

At last, Maxwell removed his fedora and shuffled back to where Tessa and Claire stood with the dogs at their feet. He spoke solemnly. "A woman died here. Recently."

The tiny blond hairs on Claire's arms stood up.

"She fell down the stairs to the basement. Her heart broke. Her neck broke in the fall. She died."

Skepticism brushed over Claire's skin. Anyone could have looked up the address of the townhouse and found news stories about Victoria Lowe. This man hadn't told them anything that wasn't in the stories, except the part about the woman's heart.

"There was a man in the house at the time."

Claire's eyes went wide.

"Angry words were tossed between them. Love slipped away and was replaced with hate." Maxwell shuddered. "The woman fell ... hard against the treads. The man went to the bottom of the stairs. He checked for a pulse. There was none. The man left the house."

Claire's face paled and she had to swallow hard to get her words out. "Did the man push her? Did the man intend to harm her?"

Maxwell glanced back at the window. "Too many feelings have mixed together. I cannot sort out the man's intention." He gave a slight bow. "I cannot stay here any longer." Leaning heavily on his cane, he struggled away up the lane.

Tessa offered her thanks to the retreating figure and when he disappeared around the corner, she looked at Claire. "I asked him to come to see if he felt what you felt when you were here previously with Nicole. I thought if he picked up on the same things, it would give you confidence in your abilities."

"What if he felt something different?" Claire asked.

"Then you could use the information as you try to learn more about Grace Dodd's death. If what Maxwell felt didn't match up with your sensations, he would have said something to you about how to better tap into your skills."

"You told him what I felt when I was here?"

Tessa shook her head. "Absolutely not. I only asked him to meet us."

"Then how would he know what I felt, if you didn't tell him?"

Tessa held Claire's eyes. "He took your hand, Claire. He shook with you. That's all he needed."

As the sun fell below the horizon and darkness descended over the alleyway, Claire looked up the lane to the corner.

Tessa said, "Maxwell didn't have any suggestions for you."

Claire turned to her about to ask a question, but Tessa spoke first. "That means to trust in your abilities. You are *not* losing them."

16

C laire leaned close to Nicole and whispered, "I don't see Dr. Dodd."

"I've been looking for him, too. I don't think he's here."

Scanning the huge crowd gathered at the gravesite, Claire searched for the husband of the woman being buried. She and Nicole stood on a slight incline at the periphery of the mourners so that they could pay their respects, but also take in the faces of the nearly one hundred people who had come to lay Grace Dodd to rest.

Vanessa stood stoically next to her younger sister occasionally lifting a tissue to her eyes. Maddy was a mess, clutching Vanessa's arm and crying into her shoulder. Claire could barely look at her ... the girl's misery and grief broke her heart.

As they rode in the cab to the cemetery, Nicole and Claire, having heard that a murderer often showed up at a funeral, decided that they would keep their eyes on the people that gathered for the service. Who knew why a killer would make such an appearance, maybe to get some sick, twisted pleasure from seeing the sadness and loss he'd created.

Claire spotted the neighbor, Lorraine Hale, who had rushed across the street the night she heard Maddy's screams. Edie Brookhaven, the house-keeper, stood alone off to the side, her face tight and drawn. Ian Fuller watched the service from a distance standing under a tall oak tree next to another man. He spotted Claire and Nicole and gave them a nod.

A woman sang a beautiful a cappella hymn and her sweet voice pulled so strongly at Claire's heart-strings that she had to bite the inside of her cheek to keep from crying. Noticing her friend reach up to brush at her eyes, Nicole took Claire's arm and moved her away from the gathering to a walkway that ran through the cemetery. "You okay?"

Claire gave a nod, but didn't say anything.

When they came to a bench, Nicole suggested they sit.

Taking in a deep breath, Claire leaned back against the seat. "Emotions bubbled up ... my mom's service ...Teddy's funeral. I wasn't expecting those feelings to hit me so hard."

"It's understandable. Little things can bring back memories." Nicole looked out over the quiet, peaceful graveyard. "Sometimes when I bake, the scent of the chocolate or the cinnamon makes me think of baking with my grandmother and then I get all teary-eyed."

"We're softies I guess." One corner of Claire's mouth turned up in a wistful smile.

Nicole asked questions about Claire's mother and Claire talked about the woman for several minutes sharing details of their lives in near poverty and how hard her mom had worked to keep a roof over their heads, and how they baked and sewed and took walks together.

"Can I ask you something without you getting angry with me?" Nicole looked sideways at her friend.

Claire chuckled. "Wow, that's a leading question. I can't make any promises about not getting angry, but I will make a guess that I'll end up forgiving whatever question you're about to ask me so go ahead."

"Teddy was in his seventies when you married him?"

"He was seventy-three."

"And you were what? Thirty-one?"

"Yes." Nicole's questions brought up old feelings of being called a gold-digger when she dated and married her husband and Claire could feel defensive feelings resurfacing.

Nicole cleared her throat. "How were you attracted to someone so much older than you? I'm just interested. I'm not accusing you of marrying for money or anything."

"Lots of people accused me of that very thing." Claire bit her lower lip, gathering her thoughts to give her friend a truthful answer. "I started working as a lawyer at Teddy's company. There was an event one evening to hear a speaker, a well-known lawyer and venture capitalist, and my department was asked to attend. I was running late and I turned the hallway corner going about sixty miles an hour. It turns out Teddy was late, too and he was hurrying to the conference room from the other direction. He turned the corner as I was rushing forward and we plowed into each other." A smile spread over Claire's lips recalling her first meeting with her future husband. "We laughed and apologized and honestly, I didn't even recognize Teddy as the founder and CEO of the company. I remember what a kind smile he gave me after the collision. We both hurried away towards the meeting room and realized we were both going to the same place. Teddy held the door for me and we went in, him to the front of the room and me to the back."

Claire sighed. "There was a reception afterwards and I was milling about with colleagues. I needed the restroom so I started to head out of the room when Teddy approached and made a joke about our crash. We ended up talking for an hour. He was funny and intelligent and down-to-earth. I enjoyed our chat, but I never thought we would meet up again."

"So what happened?"

"I was working very late one night. I was exhausted. When I was leaving, I got in the elevator and Teddy was there. His face lit up when he saw me. We chatted and when we reached the lobby, he asked if I might like to go get a coffee. He knew an all-night coffee shop around the corner. I said yes. We talked in that shop for two hours. It turned out we both came from difficult childhoods with mothers who broke their backs for us. We both loved being active, we both loved art, we had the same political leanings and passions." Claire smiled broadly. "I fell for him, I honestly fell for him ... the man himself, not who he was professionally or because of how much money he had in the bank. Teddy and I seemed cut from the same cloth. He was a gentle, kind soul who truly cared about other people."

"Just like you," Nicole grinned.

"Really?" Claire shook her head. "Sometimes I don't feel like that's me at all. I always feel that I'm not doing enough."

"So go on. He swept you off your feet?"

"We quietly dated for about six months and then he asked me to marry him. I was afraid. I was afraid I wouldn't be able to withstand the public scrutiny, the wagging tongues, the names I'd be called. It was a level of society I had no business in. I said no. Over the next few weeks, Teddy tried to calm my fears. He reminded me of how similar our backgrounds were, how much fun we had together. He knew people would be critical, but he didn't care what they said. Teddy had never been married. He told me he'd never fallen in love before. He said he was so grateful that I had come into his life." Claire took in a long breath. "I said yes."

Making eye contact with Nicole, Claire said, "I can't say that the financial security didn't cross my mind. I don't think anyone who grew up poor could help it. But, Teddy loved me and I loved him. I insisted on a prenuptial agreement. Teddy overrode the agreement in his will leaving me with enough money to live my life free from financial worries or concerns." Claire shrugged. "It's an unbelievable reversal of fortune from my early life. Now I'm filthy rich, Nic, but I hide it because I want people to like me for me."

"You...." A big smile lit up Nicole's face. "You're the anonymous donor that bought Tony's building for him so he wouldn't have to move his market."

"I'm not saying anything about that." Claire shook her head.

"It *was* you." Nicole hugged her friend. "You did that for Tony."

Claire brushed a lock of her hair out of her eyes. "I will say this. If the people around me need something, I'm going to give it to them. Teddy gave me a gift and I'm going to use it to help people."

A wicked grin spread over Nicole's face. "You

know, there's this big house on Cape Cod that I want...."

"I said *need* not *want*." Claire gave her friend a playful poke.

"Well, it seems you've been given more than one gift," Nicole said. "One tangible and one not so much."

Claire told Nicole about her meeting with the man Tessa called Maxwell. "Tessa said I wasn't losing my skills."

"That's a relief." Nicole's face looked hopeful and then she said with a grin, "Now could you just speed up the frequency and accuracy of those skills so we can get this case solved?"

Claire smiled. "Tessa told me not to push."

"I've been your friend longer," Nicole teased. "I'm telling you to push."

"I'll take that under consideration."

Nicole looked back to where they'd come from. "The service will be over soon. I wonder why Dr. Dodd didn't make an appearance."

"Maybe he couldn't face it."

"Not being here makes him look guilty."

"It does, doesn't it." Claire's blue eyes clouded. "But the man has been acting oddly and it all could be explained by high levels of grief and shock. He might be under the care of a counselor or physician who advised against attending the funeral."

"I don't buy it," Nicole huffed. "He was married to Grace for over forty years. He should be here."

"Let's head back." Claire stood and smoothed the skirt of her black dress. "We can give our condolences to Vanessa and Maddy and maybe Ian will be free for a few minutes to talk."

Nicole linked arms with Claire and they started back to the service, but when they reached the crest of the small hill and were about to walk down to join the other mourners, Claire stopped and turned her head towards a cluster of trees set back to the right of the gathering.

"Is something wrong?" Nicole asked quietly.

"I got a rush of something, a funny feeling." Claire rubbed her forehead. "It's nothing, just everything jumbling together, I guess."

Returning to the gathering, a cold tingle of anxiety gripped Claire and an unsettling thought popped into her head.

Is someone watching us from behind those trees?

17

Claire and Nicole finally made it to the front of the line to greet Vanessa and Maddy. With her eyes swollen and red from crying, Maddy stood like a zombie murmuring thanks to the people who passed by and shook her hand, all emotion drained from her. Vanessa thanked the guests, answered questions, and offered comfort, but her face was like granite and her movements stiff as if she'd banished her feelings and locked them up tight inside in solitary confinement.

When Nicole and Claire reached the young women, a tiny look of relief flitted over Vanessa's face and the tension in her muscles lessened. "I can barely stand this. I need to get out of here. I can't face going to the luncheon," she confided in a low tone. "We're both ready to collapse."

"We'll sit with you." Nicole pressed her arm. "We can act as a buffer."

"Will you ride with us in the limo?" Vanessa asked hopefully. "I have some things to tell you."

Settled in the limousine after the last of the mourners had gone through the line, Vanessa let out a moan, rested her head against the seat, and closed her eyes for a few moments. Maddy sat near the window her face turned away.

"We spoke with the Assistant District Attorney and the Greendale Police Chief." Using both hands, Vanessa pushed her hair back and cradled her face, her elbows leaning on her knees. "The blood on the upstairs woodwork is O-positive. Both my mother and father were O-positive. The blood can't be dated so they don't know how long it's been there. The investigation has enough probable cause for the prosecutor to bring it to a Grand Jury. They hope to get an indictment and bring our father to trial for manslaughter and assault and battery." Vanessa shook her head slowly. "I don't know whether to be pleased or horrified. I guess I'm both. How did this happen to our family?"

"Is your father with someone from law enforcement today?" Nicole asked.

"Not yet. They're going to see him up in Marblehead to let him know. He's still there. He doesn't even have an attorney yet." Vanessa's jaw muscle twitched. "He didn't come to Mom's funeral. Can you believe it? He digs himself a bigger and bigger hole."

Claire took a glance at Maddy who was watching out the window as the limo sped along and then she faced Vanessa. "Has the detective or the prosecutor said anything to you about Representative Lowe's death? Have they ruled it an accident?"

"I haven't heard a thing."

"He must have killed both of them." Maddy was still gazing out of the window. The fury in her voice startled Claire.

"You mean Dad?" When Vanessa put her hand on Maddy's shoulder, her sister shrugged it off.

"Yes, *him*," Maddy paused and added in a whisper, "that monster."

Claire and Nicole shared a look of concern at the anger Maddy gave off.

"Have you talked with your father recently?" Claire questioned.

Vanessa shook her head. "It's just as well."

The limo came to a stop in front of the neighborhood restaurant located less than a mile from the Dodd's home and the young women got out.

"I'm walking home. I can't go in. I've had enough," Maddy said with determination.

Vanessa was about to say something, but changed her mind. She gave her sister a hug and Maddy strode away down the sidewalk.

Claire noticed Ian standing off to the side of the parking lot speaking with a tall man wearing a suit, so she and Nicole waited. Vanessa told her friends that she would meet them inside the restaurant. When Ian and the man's conversation ended, the detective waved them over.

Ian explained, "I don't want to get close to the entrance. I'm here unofficially. The detective in charge is a friend, he asked if I'd stop by today and take a look around."

"Vanessa told us the prosecutor wants to take the case before a grand jury in order to bring Dr. Dodd to trial," Claire reported to her training partner.

"I heard that. It seems like the right thing to do."

"Was it helpful for you to be at the service?" Nicole asked.

"I was just checking over the crowd, having a

look at who was there. It doesn't often lead to anything."

"Dr. Dodd was among the missing at the cemetery." Claire made eye contact with Ian.

"I noticed. Probably not the smartest thing he could have done. The doctor isn't doing himself any favors."

"Is there any news about Representative Lowe?" Nicole asked.

Ian shifted his feet. "There's no evidence of foul play. That's off the record so keep that quiet."

Claire said, "But would there *be* any evidence if someone Ms. Lowe knew came to the townhouse and she let him in? An argument might have started, there could have been some angry words exchanged. Someone could have shoved Ms. Lowe causing her to fall down the stairs. What evidence would there be in that case?"

A smile spread over Ian's face. "I suppose that's a good point."

Ian often talked in riddles when Claire or Nicole asked him about a case he couldn't discuss.

Claire raised an eyebrow. Her ability to interpret Ian's comments was getting better. "I'm going to take that to mean the investigation into Victoria Lowe's death is on-going."

"I never said that." Ian's brown eyes brightened as he tried to suppress a smile.

"Right, and we didn't see you here today either." Nicole shook her head. "You have any other cryptic messages for us?"

"Not at the moment except that you both need to stay away from the investigation ... for your own safety." Ian's phone buzzed and he removed it from his pocket. "I mean it."

"Before you run off," Nicole said, "when we were on the hillside at the cemetery, Claire had the feeling we were being watched by someone in that group of trees that was behind where you were standing."

Claire's eyes bugged in horror that Nicole revealed to Ian what she'd sensed and told her friend before they left the cemetery.

Ian looked at Claire. "Why didn't you tell me?"

"It was only a *feeling.* I didn't see anyone."

"I'll check it out anyway." Ian started away. "I need to return this call. See you in the morning to bike," he told Claire.

When Ian was back in his car, Claire faced Nicole. "Why did you tell him that?"

"We didn't have time to check it out with the funeral service going on. I thought we should tell him."

"I'd rather not." Claire rolled her eyes. "Ian can't know about my intuition and if we're always telling him I've had a *feeling* about something, he'll think I'm crazy."

"You're right. I just thought he should know. I didn't think it through."

Claire got a faraway look on her face.

"Claire?" Nicole snapped her fingers.

Blinking, the curly-headed blonde shook herself. "Something's ... not right."

"I'll say it isn't," Nicole started to walk toward the restaurant entrance. "I haven't eaten for hours. I'm starving. Let's go into the luncheon."

"Nic." Claire hadn't moved from her spot. "Something's wrong."

Turning slowly, Nicole faced her friend with worry etched over her forehead, but before she could ask what the issue was a woman's voice called to them from the door of the restaurant. Vanessa, looking frantic, waved to the young women as she hurried down the steps and practically ran into the parking area.

The tone in Vanessa's voice chilled Claire.

"Maddy called me. She's at home. Someone broke into our house."

"Tell her to get out of the house." Claire's words

came out in a rush. "Someone could still be inside. Tell her to call the police once she's outside."

Noticing the agitated looks on the three women's faces, Ian pulled his car to a stop next to them and put the window down to hear Claire's report of trouble at the Dodd's house.

"Get in." Ian spoke into his phone as Claire, Nicole, and Vanessa climbed into the car.

A police car sped to the curb as Ian pulled up to the home. Vanessa leapt out calling for her sister. She spotted Maddy standing across the street in front of the neighbor's house and hurried to her.

"When a funeral notice gets printed in the news, it can alert robbers to an empty house," Ian said. "It's likely that's what's happened here. The officer and I will go through the place, make sure no one's inside, then we'll call in Maddy and Vanessa to take a look around, see if anything's missing."

The sisters crossed to the sidewalk in front of their house and stood with Claire and Nicole.

"Are things in disarray inside?" Claire asked Maddy.

"My father's office is." Tears glistened at the corners of Maddy's eyes. "The desk drawers are pulled out onto the floor. Papers are everywhere. I walked through the living room and into the kitchen thinking my father might be home and that maybe he had a fit in his office. I went looking for him. Nothing else was out of place."

"Maybe you disturbed a robbery in process," Nicole surmised. "Maybe the person heard you and took off out the back."

The police officer stepped out from the front door and gestured for the Dodd sisters to come into the house.

Nicole sighed. "It's just one thing after the other."

Claire stared at the stately home surrounded by the lush green lawn. "My head is spinning and you're not going to like what I'm about to say."

Nicole's eyebrows raised, but she didn't speak.

"Maddy was here right after her mother fell. Maddy was here right when the robbery was taking place. Maddy is angry as heck about her father's affair. We don't know if Maddy took a cab home after the show at the Opera House in order to get here earlier than if she'd taken the train."

"Claire...." Nicole's voice shook. "It can't be Maddy, can it?"

"Maybe she and her mother fought over whether or not to divorce the doctor. Does Dr. Dodd know that Maddy is responsible for Grace's fall from the window? Is that why he's acting so oddly? Is he trying to protect Maddy?"

"Oh, no." Nicole let out a moan. "Oh, no."

18

After the daily rush and the shop had closed for the day, Nicole, Claire, and Robby worked in the back room to fill orders for an upcoming wedding. The sweet smell of chocolate floated on the air amid the sounds of mixers whirring at full capacity.

"Why did I agree to this contract?" Nicole sighed. "I'm exhausted."

"Hang in there. We're almost done." Claire had a smudge of chocolate on her forehead.

Robby stood off to the side working at the stainless steel counter wrapping chocolate lollipops in cellophane and tying them with ribbons. He'd been unusually quiet during the hours-long process and

Claire studied his face when he wasn't paying attention trying to figure out what was going on with him. Placing the last pop in the case used for transporting the sweets to the venue, Robby stretched and rubbed his lower back. "Done," he announced.

"They look great." Nicole praised the young man. "Maybe I'll give you a bonus for staying late."

"I'll need it," Robby mumbled as he untied his apron, pulled it over his head, and tossed it into the laundry.

Claire eyed him as he walked past to get his windbreaker. "You feel okay?"

"Fine." Robby's curt reply signaled that he certainly was not fine.

"Hey." Claire rested the spoon on the counter. "What's going on?"

Nicole, aware of her young employee's somber demeanor, lifted her eyes from her task to see how Robby reacted.

Robby glanced over at Nicole. "You need a year-round, full-time employee?"

"Why? What do you mean?"

"I need a job."

"You have a job." Nicole walked around from behind the counter. "You can't go to school *and* work full-time."

"Exactly." Robby's voice was choked.

Putting her hand on his shoulder, Claire tried to pick up on what was bothering her co-worker. "Tell us what's wrong."

The skin on Robby's chin trembled and he held his lips tightly together, but then he blurted, "My mom lost her job. She can't help me with tuition. I've maxed out my loans. I won't be able to go back to school at the end of August."

Claire wrapped him in a hug as several tears escaped from the young man's eyes. "There must be a way," she said softly.

"If there is, I'd like to hear it." Robby swiped at his wet cheeks. "I'm all out of ideas."

"How much does tuition cost?" Nicole wiped her hands on a dish towel.

When Robby told her, Nicole almost fainted. "You've got to be kidding."

"I wish I was."

Nicole made quick eye contact with Claire who gave a slight nod.

"You're way too talented to give up your musical education," Claire said.

"Tell that to the financial aid office." Robby sank onto a chair.

Leaning against the counter, Claire said, "Go to

the financial aid office and tell them what happened. Talk to them about private benefactors. They might know of people who want to assist worthy students in need. If they don't, ask them to point you to an outside agency that might know of such people. Don't give up. Things have a way of working out. Go to the aid office on Monday. Be polite, but persistent. There's no way you're throwing your talent away. You need to stay in college to make contacts and learn the business side of the industry."

Robby bit his lower lip, then gave a slight nod. "I guess it's worth a try."

Nicole hugged him. "We're almost done here. Wait for us to finish. I'm taking the three of us out to dinner tonight."

A tiny grin formed on Robby's face and his reply made Claire and Nicole chuckle. "I won't refuse a free meal," he said.

Nicole playfully bopped his shoulder. "Don't get used to it."

When the work had been completed and the sweets packed away for morning delivery, the three shop workers headed to the restaurants on Newbury Street for a late night meal.

"I'm starving." Robby walked between the women as they moved along the sidewalk filled with people strolling along with friends or family. The streetlamps flickered on and the branches of trees lining the street were wrapped with twinkling white lights. The warm, clear summer evening air enveloped them.

Choosing a restaurant, they asked to be seated outside on the patio and were told there would be a wait so they headed to stand at the bar and enjoy a drink amid the congenial atmosphere of the chattering patrons.

"I'm feeling better," Robby said.

Claire smiled. "Good. Don't give up hope."

Nicole squeezed the young man in a hug. "I have a good feeling about this."

Robby looked at Claire. "Hold my hand."

Raising an eyebrow, Claire frowned. "Why?"

"Hold my hand." Robby stuck his right hand out. "Try to sense something. Tell my fortune. Do you see music in my future?"

"Come on. I can't do anything like that." Claire scoffed. "You said your grandmother had some sort of skills. Ask her."

"She's dead." Robby extended his arm towards Claire. "You sensed my secret audition last time you held my hand."

Claire blubbered something trying to brush off

her feeling about the audition as a coincidence or that she might have overheard Robby mention it, but Nicole stepped in. "Just hold his hand. Give it a try."

"Humor me," Robby grinned.

Letting out a long sigh, Claire reached for the hand that Robby held out and grasped it. She closed her eyes and hummed, 'Om,' in an attempt to make light of the situation.

"Be serious," Robby chided.

Claire went silent and tried to concentrate, but something blocked her and she felt like she needed to shake off whatever the obstacle was. An annoying buzzing played in her head. Dropping Robby's hand, she rubbed her forehead. "I can't feel anything."

Nicole eyed her friend. "Nothing?"

"Nothing about Robby."

"Do you have a headache?" Alarm showed on Nicole's face. "Is something wrong?"

Claire's head pounded and the noise in the place became almost painful to her ears. About to ask the bartender for a glass of water, Claire spotted Vanessa sitting at a high table across the room engrossed in conversation with a man.

Following Claire's gaze, Nicole spotted the woman and said with surprise, "There's Vanessa. Are you okay? We should go over to say hello."

"I don't know," Claire hesitated, but Nicole didn't hear the reluctance and started across the room weaving through the crowd.

As they approached the table, the man opposite Vanessa aggressively grabbed her wrist and when he noticed people coming near, he dropped his hand.

"Oh, hi." Vanessa blinked at the unexpected threesome and quickly placed her hand onto her lap.

"We're waiting for a table." An air of discomfort hovered around everyone and it made Nicole wish she hadn't suggested coming over to talk. "This is Robby. He works at the shop."

Vanessa appeared to recover somewhat from her surprise at seeing them at her table and she introduced her companion. "This is Matthew Adams." Even though he was sitting, the man gave the impression that he was tall. He had broad shoulders and brown hair flecked with gray cut short against his scalp. A prominent forehead and dark, heavy eyebrows emphasized his deep set, dark eyes. A serious intensity poured off of him.

Claire, estimating Matthew to be in his late forties, was the last to shake hands with him. Uncomfortable zings of electricity bit at her fingers when their skin touched and she let go. "Sorry to interrupt your conversation. We spotted you from the other side of the bar." Turning to Vanessa, she asked, "How's Maddy?"

Vanessa pushed her long dark hair over her shoulder. "She's been upset, of course. The police officer talked with her and was reassuring. The person who broke in was most likely someone who read about the funeral service and knew the house would be empty. The officer told us that it's a very common thing. Maddy must have disturbed the robber in action causing him to run off."

"I'm glad she's okay." Claire took a quick look at Matthew who appeared bored and distracted.

The man stood and said, "Excuse me," as he headed off to the restroom.

"Is everything okay?" Nicole asked gingerly.

Vanessa wouldn't make eye contact. "Yeah. I needed a break from everything. We came out for a quick drink."

"Is this the guy Maddy is unhappy about?" Claire asked.

Vanessa's face hardened. "Yes."

"Have they met yet?" Nicole questioned.

"It's too much to introduce them right now ... with everything that's going on." Vanessa took a sip from her wine glass. "I'm feeling run-down. I think we'll head out once Matthew comes back."

The restaurant buzzer went off in Nicole's purse to indicate their table was ready and she moved in to give Vanessa a hug. "I'll talk to you tomorrow. Take care of yourself. Try to get some rest."

Seated for dinner, Robby took a look across the room to where Vanessa and Matthew had been sitting. "I don't like that guy."

"Why not?" Claire kept her similar feelings to herself.

"He gave off some weirdo vibe." Robby picked up the menu. "A tough guy or some lousy boss type of person. You know, a know-it-all. He doesn't have time for peons. Too important."

"We seem to have interrupted an argument." Nicole leaned forward. "They seemed angry with each other. Did you notice how roughly Matthew gripped Vanessa's wrist?"

"What was that about?" Robby's eyebrows scrunched together. "Why is your friend with such a loser? You better step in and warn her off the guy."

With a worried expression, Nicole glanced across the table to Claire. "What did you think?"

"I think Vanessa is making a poor choice." Claire's hand still vibrated from the electrical pings she'd experienced while holding Matthew Adams's hand. "I don't think he's a very nice person."

"That's the understatement of the year," Robby moaned.

Claire couldn't have agreed more.

19

Sitting around the kitchen table eating spaghetti with the Dodd sisters and Nicole, Claire noticed a slight bruise on Vanessa's wrist where her new male friend had grabbed her the other night.

Vanessa invited them to dinner because she was worried about Maddy. The young woman had fallen into a funk and showed no interest in anything. When Vanessa broached the subject of seeing a counselor, Maddy immediately shot the idea down. Vanessa hoped that Claire and Nicole might convince her sister to change her mind.

Nicole was trying to engage Maddy in conversation by asking her about the upcoming academic year at MIT. Maddy answered politely, but her replies were short and to the point.

"I'm really not that excited about going back to school." Maddy's personality was light-years away from the person Claire had met at the Opera House. The bright light in the girl's eyes had disappeared along with her upbeat and friendly manner.

"Maybe when the time comes, you'll have more interest." Nicole smiled. "It's hard to think about school in the middle of the summer."

Maddy lifted her glass of ice water. "It's hard to think about school when your family is falling apart." The comment silenced everyone for a few minutes.

Claire dabbed her lips with her napkin and placed it next to her dinner plate. "How about we let Nicole and your sister clean up and we can go in the living room to talk?"

Maddy gave a shrug, but she left the kitchen with Claire and headed for the living room.

"What do you want to talk about?" With down-cast eyes, Maddy sank into the sofa across from Claire.

"I want to talk about loss."

"Talking isn't going to help anything."

"Sometimes, it does." Claire talked about her

mother and Teddy and the grief that nearly killed her when she lost them. "I felt lost and alone in the world ... and sometimes, I still do."

Maddy bit her lower lip and when she lifted her eyes to Claire, tears tumbled down her cheeks. "I don't know what to do."

Claire hated harboring suspicions about Maddy and whether she had been involved in her mother's death, but she had to take her uncertainty seriously. Moving to sit next to Maddy, Claire hoped to better pick up on the girl's emotions by being closer to her.

"The police will figure it out. You and Vanessa don't have to try."

"I don't know who to trust. When I see my father, I become enraged." Maddy leaned forward and put her head in her hands. "This all started because of his stupid affair. When I look at him, all I can think about is that he killed my mother."

"It might help to talk to someone who can give you ways to cope with all this."

Rubbing her forehead, Maddy muttered, "Maybe. I can't sleep, I toss and turn and when I do doze off, I dream of coming home that night, trying to talk to my father, going upstairs, standing at the window and seeing my mom outside on the ground, and then I see that person by the trees. Over and over, the same dream."

"You still think someone was out by the trees? Could it have been shadows moving?"

Maddy sat up and gazed across the room. "No. It wasn't shadows. It was a person. It was a man."

"Was the man looking up at you in the window?" Claire's heart raced.

Maddy thought. "He was looking at Mom."

"Then what happened?"

"He walked into the woods."

"Can you describe him?"

Closing her eyes, Maddy said, "It was dark. The house lights lit up part of the yard. He didn't seem old. He moved quick. He seemed tall, not heavy. I couldn't make out his face or his hair color."

"It could be a witness. It could have been someone out walking a dog. Maybe he heard the commotion coming from the house and stepped into your yard."

"I didn't see a dog." Maddy shook her head.

"You told the police all of this?"

"I think so." Maddy frowned. "I don't really remember what I told them. I don't know if I remembered all the details when I talked to them. I keep having that dream. I see the man in my dreams."

Claire knew that dreams could alter the reality of a situation and that the police might not take Maddy's claims seriously, but still. "I think you should talk to the police again and tell them what you've recalled from that night. It could help them locate the witness."

"Will they think I'm making it up?"

Anxiety flashed through Claire's body. "Why would they think that?"

"Because now I'm adding details to my story."

"I don't think that's anything to worry about."

Vanessa came into the room. "Is everything okay?"

Maddy gave a nod.

"Nicole's making popcorn," Vanessa said. "Would you two like to watch a movie?"

"That sounds good." Maddy stood and headed out of the room. "I'll go see if Nicole needs any help." Pausing at the threshold, Maddy turned back and looked at Claire. "Thanks."

With a concerned expression, Vanessa took a seat next to Claire. "Did your talk go okay?"

"It did. Maddy told me she'd consider talking to a counselor." Claire shifted a little to better face Vanessa. "She keeps dreaming about the person she saw near the tree line the night your mother died."

Vanessa let out a sigh. "Is she imagining that? How could she see in the dark?"

"Maybe we could test it out some night," Claire thought. "One of us could stand near the trees and then you could go up to the window and see what you can make out. We'd have to have similar conditions to that night. Cloud cover, moon phase, a clear night."

"Good idea." When Vanessa reached up to push a strand of hair from her face, the sleeve of her shirt slipped down her arm and the bruise on the wrist showed.

Claire swallowed hard. "Your wrist."

Vanessa tugged her sleeve into place. "I bumped it. It's nothing."

Making eye contact, Claire said with an even tone, "I saw Matthew take hold of your wrist the other night." She braced for a reaction.

"I broke off with him." Vanessa blew out a long breath. "He isn't a good match for me."

"How did he take that?" Claire expected that the man wouldn't have taken it well.

"I made sure to do it in a public place. He has a temper. He likes things a certain way. I didn't want to be alone with him when I gave him that news."

"Is he violent?"

"No." Vanessa shook her head, then modified her answer. "Matthew is used to being the boss and having everyone around him do his bidding. He doesn't seem to care about other people's feelings, only his own. He was rough with me twice, grabbed me by the arm, grabbed my wrist. I decided he wasn't for me."

"Was he angry when you said you wouldn't be seeing more of him?"

"He didn't say a word." Vanessa picked at one of her nails. "He got up calmly and left the bar. That was it."

"When did you tell him you didn't want to see him anymore?"

"I brought it up a couple of days before the funeral service. I told him I didn't think we were the right match."

"But you were with him the night we saw you at the bar."

"I alluded to not seeing him anymore prior to the funeral. The other night he called and said he wanted to talk. I met with him the night you saw us. That night was when I told him in no uncertain terms that I wouldn't be seeing him again."

"Has he contacted you since?"

"Not a word," Vanessa said. "It's actually a relief

not to have to deal with him anymore. Matthew is ... odd, and I have more than enough odd behavior with my father at the moment."

Claire was about to say something when the doorbell chimed and she and Vanessa exchanged surprised looks.

"Who could this be?" Vanessa asked, getting up from the sofa.

With Claire trailing after her, Vanessa headed for the foyer to the front door just as Nicole and Maddy entered the hall. Unlocking the heavy wooden door, Vanessa opened it to see a police officer and a man in a suit standing on the porch.

"Detective Miles." Vanessa stepped back to allow the men to enter.

"Sorry to bother," the suited man said. He took a look at Claire and Nicole, and then asked Vanessa, "Can we talk somewhere?"

"You can speak in front of our friends." Vanessa's voice shook with worry. "They're friends of Detective Fuller."

The man's face relaxed. "Are you Ian's triathlon training partner?"

Claire smiled and nodded and introduced herself. Nicole did the same.

"It's just a mini-triathlon," Claire corrected.

"Ian says he couldn't do it without you."

A pink blush covered Claire's cheeks. "That's nice of him, but I think he's exaggerating."

"Ian says you're quite an athlete." Detective Miles turned back to Vanessa. "When some things came to our attention, we decided to come by."

"What things?" Vanessa asked, her eyes wide.

Maddy moved closer to Nicole.

"The break-in of the other day," the detective said. "Some things about it seem off."

Her heart pounding, Claire stared at the man wishing he'd get to the point.

"How do you mean?" Vanessa asked.

"There was quite a lot of cash in the drawer of your father's desk. Fifty thousand dollars in cash."

Vanessa's mouth dropped open.

"Even if your sister disturbed the robber, he had plenty of time to remove the cash and take it with him."

"What are you getting at?" Vanessa's face had paled.

"We're thinking it might not have been a break-in with intent to commit a robbery."

In a hushed tone, Vanessa asked, "Why would someone break in then?"

"That can't be determined as yet."

"Why did you come to see us so late?" Maddy asked. "Why not tell us tomorrow?"

"We think it best to have a car stationed out front at night."

Vanessa sucked in an audible breath and her hand flew to her chest.

"Just for a few nights." The detective tried to gloss over his news. "To be sure everything is okay."

"What ... what do you mean?" Vanessa could barely squeeze the words from her throat. "Do you think we're in danger?"

"It's just a precaution." The detective forced a smile. "We prefer to err on the side of safety and caution. No need for alarm. It's really only standard operating procedure."

Claire didn't believe that for a second.

"The officer," the detective gestured to the police officer next to him, "will park out front. He'll arrive before dark and will leave shortly after dawn. Only for a few nights, that's all. We wanted to let you know so you wouldn't be concerned when you saw the squad car out front." The two law enforcement officers moved to the door. "Sorry to interrupt your evening."

"Should we be on guard for something?" Vanessa

stepped forward to open the door for the men. "Should we watch for anything in particular?"

"No need to do anything but your normal routine. As always, call '911' if anything seems amiss." The detective and the officer left the house.

Vanessa locked the door after them. "That isn't comforting at all. Why would we need an officer parked outside each night?"

"Like he said," Claire attempted to be reassuring, "the break-in seemed unusual so they're being cautious."

"I don't think there's anything to worry about." Nicole's voice shook when she spoke negating the intent of her words.

"Why don't we get the popcorn and settle down to watch a movie like we planned?" Claire suggested and then tried to lighten the mood by saying, "nothing can happen with a police officer right outside the door."

As they started down the hall to the kitchen to get the snacks, a shudder of cold fright ran down Claire's back. *Or can it?*

20

Claire and Ian ran along Beacon Street in the late afternoon sunshine. Suddenly Ian bolted, raced to the bottom of the hill, and turned left onto Charles Street.

When Claire caught up to him, he chuckled. "I win."

"That wasn't fair." Claire sucked in breaths of air.

Ian used the back of his hand to wipe sweat from his forehead. "It isn't fair when I take off on you, but it *is* fair when you do it to me."

"That's right." Claire grinned. "You have more muscle mass, so it isn't fair. I need a head start."

"All's fair in love and war."

When Claire's cheeks tinged pink from Ian

saying the word *love*, she was glad her face was already flushed from the heat and exercise.

As had become habit, Ian bought water bottles and they climbed the hill on Boston Common where they found a vacant bench in the shade under a huge, leafy oak tree.

"I hope the day of the triathlon is cool and overcast." Ian took a long pull on the bottle.

"You know it will be ninety degrees, sunny, and humid." Claire removed the elastic from her ponytail and let her long locks tumble over her shoulders before pushing the damp hair back and using the hair tie to push the unruly curls into a loose bun.

"It's only a week away. I think we're ready." Ian stretched his legs out in front of him and, with his eyes closed, rested his head on the bench back. "Then we should start training for next year's Boston Marathon."

"A full marathon?" One of Claire's eyebrows went up. "I don't think I could do that."

"Sure, you could. If we put in the right training time, we could definitely do it."

"Let's see how this triathlon goes next week." Claire watched the people walking and jogging through the park. "Then we can make an informed decision about our running abilities."

After ten minutes of convincing, Ian finally got Claire to agree to train for the full marathon if they both achieved a certain time goal at the upcoming athletic event.

"I was at Vanessa's house last night. Your detective friend came by."

Ian opened one eye. "Did he? Why?"

Claire explained that a police car would be stationed in front of the Dodd's house at night for the next several evenings.

Sitting up, Ian ran his hand through his hair. "Interesting."

"Why are they doing this?"

"Several possibilities. They might not be able to find Dr. Dodd and may want to intercept him should he return home."

"What's another reason?"

"They might think that someone might be planning a break-in."

A shudder ran over Claire's shoulders.

"Are Vanessa and Maddy in danger?"

Ian smiled. "Not with a squad car parked out front."

Claire elbowed the man. "I told Vanessa and Maddy that very thing, but I didn't mean it."

Ian rubbed his side where his running partner

had bopped him. "I don't know what's up. If law enforcement positioned a car at the house, they have some concerns."

Letting out a sigh, Claire asked, "Do you think Dr. Dodd killed his wife?"

"I don't have access to the investigation, so I can't say."

"Maddy is sure she saw someone near the trees at their property line the night her mom was killed. She dreams about it every night. If someone was there, he or she might have witnessed Mrs. Dodd's fall. I told Maddy she ought to speak to the police about the details she's recently recalled." Claire took a swig of her water. "Do you think dreams interfere with accurate recall of an incident?"

"Most of the time, yeah," Ian said. "Dreaming about an event, thinking about it endlessly can alter the mind's image of the situation. But, sometimes, and this happens rarely, letting the mind work on it can bring details to the forefront that someone glossed over initially."

"Would hypnosis help?"

"It might, but it wouldn't hold up in court."

Claire watched a woman sit down on a bench several yards away. The woman's little dog took a few running jumps and at last, made it onto the seat to settle next to his owner. "I saw Dr. Dodd here on the Common a couple of days after Mrs. Dodd died. We'd finished up a training run. You'd just left."

Ian looked at Claire in surprise. "He was here?"

"He works at the hospital." She gestured over the hill. "He was sitting on that bench over there."

"Was he alone?"

"No, there was another man with him. Whatever they were discussing, they seemed very serious about it."

"Interesting."

"I took a picture of them."

Ian's eyebrows raised.

"I showed it to Vanessa. She didn't know who the guy was."

"Do you still have it?" Ian straightened up.

"Yeah." Claire reached for the phone in her arm band holder and flipped through the photos until she found the one she wanted. "Here they are."

Ian held the phone, brought his face close to the screen, and his eyes widened. "I know this guy."

Claire's jaw dropped.

"He's a private investigator. He doesn't do much anymore, occasionally he takes on a client."

"Why would he be talking to Dr. Dodd shortly after Grace Dodd died?"

"Good question."

Claire offered a possibility. "Maybe the men are friends."

Ian made eye contact with Claire.

"It's possible, isn't it?" Claire gave a shrug. "What's the guy's name?"

"Bob Cooney." Ian tilted his head. "Don't get any ideas about talking to him."

"Why not?" Claire asked.

"Because this case is a mess. You and Nicole need to stay out of it." Ian's jaw muscle tightened. "If something happened to you...." He cleared his throat. "Then who would I train with?"

"I bet you could find someone."

Ian held Claire's eyes. "I like training with you."

A warm flush ran through Claire's body and she tried to deflect the feeling by asking, "Is that because you like beating me when we race each other down Beacon Street?"

A smile spread over Ian's lightly tanned face. "Yes."

The two chatted for a few more minutes about the case and then discussed their training schedule for the rest of the week.

"I'd better get going." Claire stood and stretched

her arms over her head. "I need to get the dogs from Tony. See you in the morning?"

"You bet." Ian started up the walkway towards the gold-domed State House. "Stay out of trouble."

Claire smiled and waved and headed to Tony's market hoping Augustus might be there for his afternoon coffee. When she opened the door, Bear and Lady hurried over to greet her wiggling with joy to see their owner. Claire patted the two happy Corgis and lifted her head to see Tessa standing next to Augustus's table.

"Hi." Tessa's face lit up when she saw Claire. "I came by to pick up a couple of things on the way home from work."

Claire gave the woman a hug. "Where's Tony?"

"I talked him in to going for a walk with me. He's gone to change."

"Tony? A walk?" Claire's face looked blank. "Is he feeling okay?" she kidded.

Tessa's laugh sounded like a tinkling bell. "Is a walk out of the ordinary for him?"

Claire and Augustus exchanged a look and said in unison, "Yes."

"I walk." Tony's voice boomed from the store room as he came out dressed in pressed chinos and a light blue buttoned-down shirt. His silver-gray hair had been carefully combed.

Claire smiled at the tall husky man. "You look nice."

"Shall we?" Standing across the room near the door, Tessa's eyes sparkled at the store owner.

As Tony passed by Claire on the way out of the deli-market, she winked at him and whispered, "No kissing on the first date."

Tony rolled his eyes at Claire, gave his employee some instructions about what needed to be done, walked over to Tessa with a joyful expression on his face, and opened the door for her. The two stepped out into the late afternoon sunshine.

Claire sank into the seat opposite Augustus. "Well, well. Someone looks bright-eyed and bushy-tailed, doesn't he?"

"Indeed, he does." A little smile played over the older man's mouth. "It is a pleasant sight to see Tony so happy. That said, tomorrow morning, I plan to tease him mercilessly about his crush on the woman."

"Wait until I get here." Claire smiled a wicked grin. Getting herself a tea from the little coffee bar, she returned to her seat. "I was hoping you were still here. I have a bunch to tell you." Claire proceeded to report all that had gone on over the past days related to Grace Dodd and her fall from the window.

Augustus listened with interest, asking an occasional question, but allowing Claire to lay all the information out for him.

"I admit I got scared when the detective told us they were placing a police car outside the Dodd's house. I was glad to get back home to my own place." Claire rested her chin in her hand. "Do you have any news from your contacts about the case?"

Augustus put his coffee mug on the small rickety table. "Some. Not much. Conjecture, at best."

Claire waited for some details.

"There are some rumors going around that Dr. Dodd was seen going into Victoria Lowe's townhouse on the morning of her death. It is believed Dr. Dodd had a key to her home."

Claire sat straight. "Did he? So he went in and what? They argued? He pushed her down the stairs?"

"Dr. Dodd told the police that he had nothing to do with Ms. Lowe's death."

"He told the police he was in her house? How can he prove he didn't hurt her?"

"The coroner pinpointed the death within a

window of four hours. Dr. Dodd arrived at the woman's house within that window."

"That means he could have killed her."

"It also means he may not have."

Claire exhaled loudly. "They didn't find any evidence in the house that could point to Dodd as the killer?"

"His fingerprints are all over the place." Augustus lifted his mug and sipped. "Not surprising since he was having an affair with the woman."

"Where are the answers?" Claire leaned back in exasperation. "This thing is going around in circles. Wait." She pulled out her phone. "Look at this picture. Ian told me the man with Dr. Dodd is a private investigator named Bob Cooney."

Augustus took a close look and returned the phone. "Ian is correct."

"You know Cooney?" Claire's eyes widened.

"I know who he is. I don't believe he does much investigating these days, but if the money was right...."

"Why would Dr. Dodd be meeting with an investigator?"

"They could be friends," Augustus said. "But I doubt it. Cooney isn't quite the right social match for Dr. Dodd."

"So you think it was a *professional* meeting? Maybe the doctor hired him for something?"

"If I was a betting man, I might wager that Dr. Dodd paid Cooney for his skills."

"What's this Cooney like?" Claire narrowed her eyes. "What kind of skills does he have?"

"Remember I have never met the man." Augustus tilted his head and looked Claire in the eyes. "My understanding is that Cooney is not always ethical in the jobs he takes. He does do work for insurance companies investigating fraud, but he also does other things. He's careful. Nothing sticks to him."

"What do you mean *other* things?"

"Drug dealing, some high-paying jobs in white collar crime. This is all through the grapevine, of course."

"If I talked to him, would he tell me things or would he keep client confidentiality?"

Augustus tried to suppress a smile. "Investigators are not required to maintain confidentiality unless doing work for a lawyer who is bringing a case to court. Even if he was obliged, I don't believe Mr. Cooney would hold to keeping a confidence."

"How can I find him to strike up a conversation?

Do you know anyone who could point me in the right direction?"

"I do. Me. Mr. Cooney is known to have a drink each day at 4pm." Augustus told Claire the name of the bar in the South End where the man could be found.

"He's there every day?"

Augustus nodded.

"You think he'd talk to me?"

"Without question."

"I think I might pay a visit to that bar someday." Claire grinned. "I've never been there before."

"Take Nicole with you." Augustus cleared his throat. "Mr. Cooney fancies himself a ladies' man. I wouldn't want you to be alone when you strike up a conversation with him." The former judge leveled his eyes at the young woman sitting across from him. "Be on your guard, Claire."

21

Wearing summer dresses and with their long hair falling over their shoulders, Claire and Nicole entered the bar-pub at 4:30pm and the establishment was a far cry from the rundown, seedy place they expected. The place had brick walls with carefully chosen artwork, polished wood floors, a granite bar, bottles lined up on shelves running along a wall of mirrored glass. The vibe was warm and welcoming. A few people sat at wooden tables scattered around the room and several men and women perched on bar stools.

Noticing that the man they'd come to find was sitting at the bar, Claire nodded at Nicole and they headed over.

"Are these taken?" Claire smiled at the thin, wiry man wearing a fitted dark blue shirt and black slacks.

When Bob Cooney turned away from his conversation with the bartender to see who had spoken to him, his eyes brightened when he saw the two young women standing next to him. "Absolutely not, please have a seat."

The bartender took the girls' orders.

"Bob," Cooney introduced himself.

Claire and Nicole told the man their first names.

"Names as lovely as the women they belong to." A wide smile showed perfect white teeth against the sun-tanned face. Cooney had dark brown eyes and jet black hair, but not a single gray strand showed in the thick locks and Claire guessed the fifty-something man must get his hair dyed. "What brings you to the South End?"

"Shopping, mostly." Nicole took a sip from the drink the bartender had placed in front of her.

"Tourists or locals?" Cooney asked.

"Locals," Nicole told the man. "Although Claire has only been here for a year and a half."

Cooney made eye contact with Claire and the look on his face gave her a feeling of distaste. "Where'd you come from?" the man asked.

"I lived in New York and on Nantucket." Claire forced a smile.

"Nice places. What brought you to Boston?"

"I needed a change." Claire shifted in her chair to better face Cooney. "How about you? Local?"

"Born and bred." Cooney took a long swallow from his beer glass, allowing his eyes to linger over Claire's body.

The conversation covered the pros and cons of living in the city, local politics, the weather, and what they did for a living - Cooney told them he did consulting ... and then Nicole brought up the suspicious deaths of Grace Dodd and Victoria Lowe. "Any guesses as to what's going on?"

Cooney exuded bravado helped along by his consumption of alcohol and he latched onto the subject Nicole brought up, clearly intending to impress the young women. "I know the guy."

"Dr. Dodd?" Claire asked with mock surprise.

"Yeah. I did some work for him."

"What sort of work?"

"I'm also a private investigator." A smug smile crossed Cooney's mouth.

Claire and Nicole leaned forward with interest.

"Really?" Claire said. "I've never met an investigator."

Nicole asked, "You did some sort of investigative work for Dr. Dodd?"

"The guy's a piece of work. Not bad looking for an older gent, I guess, but really not any great shakes in the looks department. The guy's kind of flabby, probably from years of doing nothing but hunching over a patient, but I guess money talks. The doc is loaded, made tons of money in investments." Cooney's eyes sparkled. "The old doc has plenty of extracurricular activities to keep him busy, if you know what I mean."

Nicole's eyes widened. "What do you mean? He was having more than one affair?"

"I don't think you'd label his escapades as *affairs*. He had the one affair going with the Lowe woman. What she saw in the doc I can't even guess. She was loaded, too, so is her husband. Anyway, the doc is a busy man, likes to go to the bars and pick up women. He has an apartment in the city." Cooney chortled. "I'm sure the wife didn't know how many visitors her husband was entertaining."

Afraid to inhibit Cooney's revelations, Claire and Nicole stifled their impulse to rail against how disgusting the doctor and his activities were. Instead, Claire showed interest by saying, "It's like a movie or a television show. Full of intrigue and suspense."

Cooney responded to Claire's comment. "I don't know how the guy had time to work." Shaking his head in almost an admiring way, he went on. "Then comes the wife's death and on top of that, the death of the woman he's been seeing on the side. The doc knows how to get himself into trouble. Dumb dope, he had it made in the shade until these two things happened."

The bartender brought over another round of drinks.

"What work did you do for Dr. Dodd?" Claire asked, hoping to get some specifics.

"The doc was sure his wife was cheating on him. Isn't that rich? The pot calling the kettle black. Anyway, he wanted me to investigate his wife, see what she was up to."

"*Was* she having an affair?" Nicole asked eagerly to keep Cooney talking.

"Nah. The doc imagined the whole thing. The woman was straight as an arrow. Maybe he hoped she was fooling around, too. Maybe in his mind that would excuse his busy lifestyle." Cooney stared into his beer glass for a moment. "I get the feeling the doc isn't that mentally stable."

Claire asked, "Why do you say that?"

Cooney looked up and gave a shrug. "He says

crazy things like suspecting the wife of an affair." The man shook his head. "He told me he thought someone was after him."

Sitting at attention, Claire questioned, "What? Who?"

"The doc said someone wanted to hurt him ... for something he'd done."

"Maybe one of the women he was stringing along." Nicole snorted. "I'd think he might have an army of women who would love to hurt him."

"Not a woman. The doc always said 'he.'"

"What did he say about the person?"

"He'd mutter stuff like 'I know he's out to get me.' I asked if he wanted me to look into it and he nearly jumped down my throat. He told me to stay out of it, it would only make it worse."

"You think he was imagining it?" Nicole asked.

"Who knows," Cooney said. "I wouldn't be surprised. The guy seemed distracted, paranoid."

"You met with him before and after Mrs. Dodd died?"

"Yeah."

"Did he act strangely before his wife died or only afterwards?"

"Both." Cooney chuckled. "I sure wouldn't want him doing any surgery on me. The guy was violent, too. He claimed he and the missus had plenty of fights."

Nicole leaned forward. "Physical fights?"

"Yeah." Cooney gave a nod. "The doc had cuts on the sides of his face and I asked what happened to him. He told me his wife did it. I laughed and that seemed to annoy him. He told me they had regular arguments that ended with the two of them using each other as punching bags. Sounds like a barrel of laughs, doesn't it?"

"What were they fighting about?" Claire asked.

"The wife found out about the affair. The good doctor had been hiding money away for years. The wife found out, I guess. She was planning to divorce him, but was biding her time to get the finances in order."

Claire's heart beat sped up. "Do you know that from your investigation into Mrs. Dodd?"

"Yeah."

"Did you report that to Dr. Dodd? That his wife knew he'd been hiding money?"

"Of course, that's what I got paid to do."

"When did you tell him she knew about the money?"

"The day before she died."

They were quiet for almost a full minute, and

then Claire asked, "Do you think Dr. Dodd killed his wife?"

One of Cooney's eyebrows went up. "I wouldn't be surprised."

"Did you know the doctor before he hired you to look into his wife's activities?" Nicole hoped Cooney knew the doctor before Mrs. Dodd discovered her husband's affair and financial manipulations because she wanted to know if he'd thought the doctor's behavior had changed over time.

"I only met the guy when he wanted to hire me."

"How did he find you?"

"There's plenty of ways to find what you want. Ask around, you end up finding what you need. It ain't hard."

Claire asked, "Did the police question you about Dr. Dodd?"

Cooney sat upright and narrowed his eyes. "Nah. The cops don't know I dealt with the doc. All my work is done strictly in cash. I meet with clients outside. We make our arrangements verbally. No cell phone, no email. No trace." The man's lips turned up at the corners. "You gotta know how to run a business."

"I guess that's true," Nicole said.

As Cooney drained his glass, he let his eyes rove

over Nicole's chest. "Enough gibbering about that old goat. He'll get what he deserves. How about I take you two lovely ladies to dinner? My treat." Cooney leaned close and his boozy breath almost made Claire recoil. He leered at the young women. "Then after dinner, maybe, who knows? I could show you my place."

Nicole's face paled at the thought. "It's been nice talking with you, but we're already late to be somewhere."

"It can't be more important than this." Cooney smiled. "Want some company?"

"I don't think you'd enjoy it." Claire fibbed, "We have to go take care of Nicole's aunt. She's bedridden. Her caretaker needed the night off."

A look of distaste covered Cooney's face. "Well, aren't you two angels of mercy. Bless your hearts." He nodded. "Nice to talk to you." The man got up and headed to the end of the bar where a group of attractive young women were laughing and talking.

"I guess we've been dismissed." Claire rolled her eyes. "Anyway, we got some information. Mission accomplished."

"Thank heavens." Nicole slid off the stool. "Let's get out of here. I've had quite enough of Mr. Cooney."

22

Nicole drove along the quiet streets of Greendale as Claire watched out the window at the houses shrouded in darkness. Bear and Lady sat in the backseat of the car each one looking out with their noses sniffing the evening smells coming into the vehicle through the slight openings at the top of the windows. During the ride to the Dodds' house, the young women had been going over the conversation they'd had with Bob Cooney trying to figure out what it might mean for the case and they decided not to discuss Cooney or his findings with Vanessa or Maddy just yet.

"Dr. Dodd sounds like he's losing it." Nicole turned the wheel of the rental car to head down a side street. "Cooney made him sound crazy and paranoid."

"Something's wrong with the man," Claire agreed. "His insatiable need to be with so many women points to some desperate need in him that can never be fulfilled."

Nicole smiled and kidded her friend. "I didn't know you'd studied psychiatry."

Claire chuckled. "It seems like common sense. Striving to be the best, entering a demanding field, the desire to accumulate wealth, the need to attract women, it all seems to spell out a man who needs constant adulation and attention. He must have a hole inside of him that can never be filled."

"All of that would be really sad if Dodd's behavior wasn't so awful." Nicole sighed as she pulled into the driveway of the Dodd house and headed to the end of the long drive around the back of the house. "There's the police car."

Claire shook her head. "Having that squad car parked out front only serves to make me nervous. Its presence is not comforting at all."

The Corgis led the way to the front door and before Claire could press the bell, the door flew open. Vanessa stood before them, her eyes looking tired and her mouth pulled down. "My father was here."

The group stepped into the foyer.

"Was he?" A shiver of unease ran down Claire's back. "Did he speak to you?"

"Maddy got home early from MIT because she had a dentist appointment in town. I've been having her stay at my apartment in Cambridge while I'm at work and sometimes she goes over to MIT. We come back here together. I don't want her alone in this house all day."

Nicole asked, "Isn't the housekeeper here during the day?"

"My father let her go shortly after Mom's accident." Creases lined Vanessa's forehead and her skin had lost its healthy glow. The stress was taking its toll on her.

They moved into the kitchen where Maddy was standing at the counter eating a sandwich. She offered to make one for Claire and Nicole, but they declined. The Corgis eagerly accepted pieces of chicken from Maddy and a broad smile spread over the young woman's lips. "I'm glad you brought the dogs."

Vanessa sank heavily onto one of the kitchen

chairs. "Our father was here when Maddy got home."

Claire glanced to the girl. "What did he say?"

Leaning against the counter, Maddy folded her arms over her chest. "I was surprised to see him. His car wasn't here. When I heard him in the office, I thought it was another break-in. He told me he parked on the street behind the trail that goes past our house in the back. When I asked him why, he said it was safer." A few tears glistened in Maddy's eyes. "I asked if he was going to stay at home now. He shook his head and said he didn't want to put us in danger. I asked what he meant. He didn't answer."

"Why did he come back here?" Nicole tilted her head.

"He had a briefcase on the desk. I think he filled it with cash."

Claire's thoughts were racing. The doctor must have several stashes of cash in the office. He mustn't want to use credit cards to keep his whereabouts secret. But why? What does he mean not wanting to put his daughters in danger? Is he losing his grip on reality or is something else at play?

"Did he tell you where he's staying?" Claire asked. She wished she'd asked Bob Cooney if he knew where the doctor had an apartment in Boston.

"I didn't think to ask."

"Was he here when you got home?" Nicole directed the question to Vanessa.

"He was just about to leave. He said he was sorry. He said he loved us." Vanessa cleared her throat. "Dad told us he wanted us to be safe. He was sweating and acting all nervous. Then he took off out the back with his briefcase."

In a gentle tone of voice, Claire asked, "When he talks about you two being safe ... do you think he worries that he's becoming unhinged and that's why he doesn't stay at home? Is he worried he'll do something to hurt you?"

Vanessa closed her eyes for a few seconds. Her breathing was quick and shallow. "I don't know anything. For a minute, I almost felt bad for him, but the emotion evaporated as soon as I thought about what he'd done to our family. I don't think I can ever forgive him."

The room was deathly quiet for a few minutes until Maddy broke the silence. "I'm sick of talking about him. Let's go ahead with what we planned."

Vanessa blew out a long breath and stood. "It's earlier than the night Mom died, but it's dark enough so I think it will work. Maddy and Claire will go up to the third floor. Nicole and I will go outside together and one of us will stand where Maddy remembers seeing the figure that night. Give us a few minutes to get into position before you look out the window."

Maddy moved to the light switch panel on the kitchen wall near the rear door to the yard. "I'll put the back light on like it was that night. Go out the back door so the police officer doesn't see you and wonder what we're doing."

Claire, Maddy, and the Corgis went to the foyer to climb the staircases to the third floor. When they were about to enter the bedroom where Mrs. Dodd fell from the window, Claire noticed the blood on the woodwork hadn't yet been removed.

"The light was off that night so we'll keep it off now." Maddy sat down on the bed and the dogs jumped up and leaned against her causing Maddy's facial expression to soften. She ran her hands over the animals' soft coats. "I wish I had a dog."

"I bet you'll get one day," Claire said with a warm smile. Turning her gaze to the window, she could see a few stars glimmering in the night sky and thought how peaceful the evening looked. "It's probably time. Shall I open the window?"

Maddy nodded and Claire pushed the sash up so that the glass and the window screen were out of the way. A gust of warm air blew into the room pushing at the light drapes to lift them up. They settled back into place with a flutter.

"All set." Claire stepped back.

Maddy moved her feet slowly over the wood floor to the window. Pushing her shoulders back, she leaned forward and looked down to the lawn. Her breath caught in her throat and her hand flew up to cover her mouth as she stared at the place on the dark grass where her mother had fallen. Maddy put her other hand on the window frame and turned her head slightly to the rear property line. "I can see Nicole," Maddy whispered and stepped away from the window.

Letting out barks, the dogs leapt from the bed and rushed to Claire jumping around her legs. "Hush, you two." Claire took the young woman's place at the window and watched the person in the yard start moving towards the house. "I see her, too. She's coming back in now."

Putting her arm around Maddy's shoulder, Claire said, "I can't imagine how hard it was to relive that night."

Still barking, Bear and Lady tore from the room and galloped down the stairs. Claire shook her head and called after them. "It's just Nicole and Vanessa coming in from the yard."

Suddenly, zips of electricity bit into her arm and images flashed in her mind of a dark figure moving across the lawn. Claire pulled her arm from Maddy's shoulders just as Nicole screamed their names from the first floor.

When Claire and Maddy reached the foyer, Nicole babbled at them about a rope.

"What are you saying?" Claire asked gently. "I don't understand."

Nicole pulled Maddy and Claire to the kitchen to see Vanessa standing next to a coil of rope lying on the floor. Vanessa pointed and Claire, with her heart in her throat, inched over to see the thing.

"My God." Vanessa could barely squeeze the words out. "Was someone in here?"

The dogs let out woofs and ran about with their noses pressed to the floor while Maddy grabbed a knife from the kitchen drawer. "Call the police."

"I'll go get the officer from his car." Claire turned on her heel.

"Don't go alone." Nicole hurried after Claire. "We stay in pairs. I'll come with you."

Once out on the front porch, Claire waved at the squad car. "Sir! We need some help." When the man didn't respond, she and Nicole strode across the lawn with the dogs bounding ahead howling. "He must have fallen asleep," Claire muttered.

Just as she raised her hand to knock on the driver side window, Claire stopped with her fist in mid-air. Under the streetlight, she could see the officer slumped in his seat at an odd angle. Something had spattered over the windshield.

Blood.

Claire caught the scream as it tried to escape from her throat.

The officer was dead.

23

Claire sat at the small table in the market telling Tony and Augustus what had happened at the Dodd house the prior evening. Bear and Lady had gone out to the walled-in, back garden off the storage room where they lounged in the grass enjoying the cool, early morning air.

"The officer was dead. I can't get the image of him slumped over in the car out of my head."

"It'll be okay, Blondie." Tony reached over and rubbed Claire's shoulder and she lifted her hand to squeeze his.

"We were at the house for over two hours while the police questioned us and examined the place." Claire shook her head. "Bear and Lady tried to alert me to the intruder, but I thought they were excited because they heard Nicole and Vanessa returning to the kitchen."

Tony's face was drawn and serious. "It's a good thing you didn't go downstairs when the guy was in the house. You could have been killed."

Augustus nodded. "The officer had already been attacked before the man broke in. It was a very good thing that you brought Bear and Lady with you. The barking of the dogs probably scared the perpetrator off. This man was most likely the one who broke in and went through Dr. Dodd's office on the day of Mrs. Dodd's funeral. He's probably watched the house on a number of occasions and had never seen dogs before. When he heard the barking, he must have realized that there were more people in the house than just Vanessa and Maddy."

"I'm thankful for those two wonderful dogs," Claire said. "They've saved me from trouble more than once." She hesitated, but then said, "I'm worried that the person who killed the officer and broke into the house is Dr. Dodd."

Tony's eyes bugged. "The doctor?"

Claire directed her next comment to Augustus. "I met with the private investigator yesterday. Dr. Dodd *did* hire him."

Tony sat up straight. "What private investigator? What did I miss?"

Taking out her phone, Claire showed Tony the picture of Dr. Dodd and the investigator sitting together in the Boston Common. "I saw these two after I did a training run. It was shortly after Grace Dodd died. Ian recognized the guy and Augustus knew where he was every afternoon so I went to talk to him. His name is Bob Cooney."

Tony's cheeks flushed. "You went to see this guy? I'm glad I didn't know you went to see him. I'd have been a wreck. You need to be more careful. Who knows what a guy like that is like, what he's up to?"

"Augustus knew. Nicole came with me. He was kind of a creep, but we got some information from him." Claire told her companions what she'd learned. "The most important details were that the doctor keeps an apartment in the city and used it with the women he picked up. Cooney told us that Dodd was ... promiscuous."

"What a loser," Tony spat the words out, disgusted by the doctor's behavior.

"Cooney also told us that the doctor was paranoid. He told the investigator that someone was after him."

"Delusional, perhaps?" Augustus guessed. "The

doctor's world is collapsing. His wife discovered his affair, she died under strange circumstances, his lover died in her townhouse under strange circumstances. Whether or not the doctor is responsible for the deaths or not, the man has lost command of his life and may be spinning out of control."

"If he didn't kill those women, then what happened to them?" Tony asked.

"I suppose Grace could have jumped." Claire absent-mindedly swirled the liquid around in her mug. "She was under stress. She and her husband fought frequently. Their fights were physical. It might have been too much for her."

"And the lover?" Tony asked. "What happened to her?"

Claire shrugged. "Maybe she tripped and fell down the stairs?"

"Dr. Dodd is thought to have entered the woman's townhouse the day she died," Augustus told Tony.

"Okay, then," Tony said. "My vote is that the doctor killed both of them."

Resting her chin in her hand, Claire sighed. "If that's the case, then Dr. Dodd must have been the one who trashed his own office in some kind of a fit." As anxiety gripped Claire's stomach, she lifted her head and made eye contact with the men sitting with her. "And he must have returned to the house last night, killed the officer, and had plans to murder his daughters."

"For God's sake." Tony shook his head. "The police need to take Dodd in for a psychological examination. He's gone off his rocker. Get him off the streets ... and he shouldn't still be practicing medicine, either. The man needs help. Why won't someone help him?"

Tony's words kept pinging in Claire's head, but she couldn't figure out why.

"Are Vanessa and Maddy still at home?" Lines of concern furrowed Tony's forehead. "They shouldn't stay there alone."

"They left their house for a while," Claire said. "The police didn't think they should go to Vanessa's apartment so they're staying with me."

"Good," Tony said, but then his eyebrows shot up. "With you? Is that a good idea? Won't they put you at risk by staying with you? Can't they stay in a hotel for a few days?"

"I have an extra bedroom, Nicole doesn't, so I offered." Claire gave a tired smile. "At a time like this, it's better to be around other people. Anyway, my place has better security than any hotel." After

Claire's townhouse had been broken into last month, she asked the building owners to invest in a security system and they agreed.

Tony didn't look satisfied, but he didn't say any more about it.

Feelings of hopelessness surrounded Claire, and she wanted to shift the conversation away from the case so she turned to Tony. "So how was your walk with Tessa the other day?"

A smile formed over Augustus's face as he waited for Tony's reply.

The big man's cheeks turned red and he muttered, "It was too hot."

Claire couldn't believe Tony had just made the perfect opening for her so she smiled and asked innocently, "Was that because of the weather or because you were with Tessa?"

Tony groaned and pushed away from the table. "Some of us have work to do."

Augustus and Claire chortled with delight.

"You two can leave anytime you want, you know." Tony growled from behind the counter which only served to make Claire and Augustus laugh harder.

When a few customers entered the store, Claire collected herself and stood. "I better get going. I want to stop at the townhouse before I go to work. If I don't hurry, Nicole will fire me."

As she was about to leave, Augustus said, "Claire, you know I have many friends in this town. If you need anything, just call me."

Claire took in a breath and nodded.

Augustus held her eyes pointedly. "Be safe."

VANESSA WAS in the kitchen preparing breakfast when Claire got home.

"Did you find everything you need?" Claire asked.

Vanessa gave her friend a hug. "Yes. Thanks again for giving us safe harbor. I really didn't want to go to a hotel. It makes me feel better knowing you have a security alarm here." She returned to the stove where she was cooking eggs for her and Maddy's breakfast. "I can't believe my parents never installed one at the house."

Maddy was sitting outside at the patio table and waved at Claire through the glass doors.

Claire returned the wave while she packed her lunch into a small cooler bag. "You're welcome to stay as long as you like. The dogs are at Tony's market. I'll pick them up on the way home from work. Are you going into the office today?"

"I feel like it's best to keep to a regular schedule. Maddy's going to MIT to meet with a professor. I'll pick up some things at the market later so I can cook dinner for all of us tonight."

Claire smiled. "We can take turns. I'll cook tomorrow night."

Vanessa checked the wall clock. "I'm late. I'd better hurry." Using a spatula, she divided the eggs between two plates and called to Maddy that the food was ready. As she lifted a forkful of the eggs into her mouth, Vanessa unzipped a jewelry case that she'd placed on the kitchen island and removed a pair of hoop earrings.

Something in the case caught Claire's eye. "That's a beautiful watch."

Vanessa stared sadly at the rose-gold watch with a soft, brown leather band. "It was my father's. He gave it to me when I graduated college. It belonged to his father."

"Can I look at it?" Claire was drawn to the piece and took it from Vanessa when she passed it to her. "It's lovely."

Suddenly, the watch seemed to be heating up in Claire's hand and her vision turned red for a moment. Zips of electricity bit at her fingers so fiercely that she let the watch slip from her hand.

Vanessa ate another bite of egg while she put on her earrings. "After everything that's happened with my father, I can't wear that watch anymore. I can barely stand to look at it."

With her heart pounding, Claire's head spun and her hand trembled from touching the timepiece. She let her arm fall to her side so Vanessa wouldn't notice it shaking. Stepping back from the island, she said, "I need to get to the chocolate shop. I'll see you later."

Claire hurried out of the townhouse as quickly as she could. She had to get away from that watch.

24

The chocolate shop buzzed with customers for most of the day keeping Claire, Nicole, and Robby busy filling take-out orders and waiting on people at the tables. It was nearly 3pm when there was finally a lull in the activity and they hurried about refilling the pastry cases, running the dishwasher, and popping some sweets into the ovens to bake.

The lovely smell of baking chocolate cookies filled the air. Claire sliced a marble cheesecake into pieces while Robby ran the big mixer and Nicole carried in a tray with three lattes on it so they could have a few minutes for a break.

"I really need to hire some more help." Nicole lifted her cup to her lips.

"You won't need to do that when I'm working full-time all year round." Robby's face was glum.

"Have you talked to the financial aid office?" Claire asked. "Were they able to help you find funding?"

"I think it's a lost cause." Robby took his cup back to the work table.

"Don't you give up hope," Nicole told him as she eyed Claire.

"I'll take care of it," she whispered to Nicole. "He isn't going to drop out of school."

"Thank heavens." Nicole spoke softly so that Robby wouldn't hear.

Claire gestured with her head for Nicole to meet her in the front of the shop and they both left the back room.

An expression of worry was written all over Nicole's face. "I knew it. You were quiet all morning. What's wrong?"

Before Claire could say anything, the shop door opened and Vanessa strode inside, her jaw tight and her eyes blazing. "I'm down this way to meet a client. I thought I'd come by and pick up an iced coffee to take with me."

"Is something wrong?" Seeing the young

woman's manner and expression, Nicole knew that something was bothering Vanessa.

"I have a million things to do." Vanessa put down her briefcase and sighed. "The air-conditioning feels good in here."

While Claire moved behind the counter to make the beverage, she kept her eyes glued to their friend.

Vanessa's phone buzzed, but she didn't reach for it.

"I think your phone just got a message," Nicole said.

Vanessa let out a groan. "As if I don't have enough trouble in my life."

A shiver of chilly air seemed to run down Claire's back.

"That pest has been hounding me." Vanessa's words dripped with annoyance. "I knew it was too convenient for him to accept what I said and leave me alone."

"Who?" Nicole asked.

"Matthew. He's been pestering me. Texts, phone calls. He wants to talk. He thinks he should try again. He cares about me. I won't answer and I don't respond and the calls increase in frequency until I text and tell him that it won't work between us. He goes quiet for a few hours and then it all starts again."

"Block him on your phone," Nicole suggested.

Vanessa didn't say anything.

"Don't you want to?"

Vanessa reached for her bag and grabbed her phone. She punched at the screen with her index finger with such force that Nicole thought it would break. "There. I did it."

"Why didn't you do it before?" Nicole questioned.

Vanessa sucked in a long breath. "I was nervous about it. I get the idea that Matthew doesn't often get told *no*. I thought blocking his calls could set him off. I just want to be left alone."

"Did you worry he'd come to your apartment or something?" Nicole eyed her friend.

"No, I was so worked up about everything I let my mind run away with silly ideas." Vanessa gave a weak smile. "Since we moved out and we're staying at Claire's now, I don't even have to think about it anymore."

Claire brought over the iced coffee and Vanessa stood up and gathered her things. "I'll see you tonight."

"Jeez. Some people. Why can't they take no for

an answer and move on?" Nicole asked wearily. "Now tell me what's bothering *you*."

Claire sat down at the café table with Nicole and explained how she felt when holding Vanessa's watch that morning. "It used to belong to her father."

Nicole's hand moved to her throat. "Why did that happen? What does it mean?"

"I don't know." Claire kneaded the back of her neck. "At first, I thought my hand hurt because Dr. Dodd used to wear the watch, but the sensation got much stronger and my vision went black ... not exactly black, sort of reddish, and I felt dizzy and almost sick."

"Oh, no." Nicole moved her hand from her throat to the side of her face. "It's your intuition trying to send you some kind of a message, isn't it?"

"I have no idea what it means, but I've felt anxious and worried ever since it happened." Claire clutched her hands together and rested them on the tabletop. "I'm not sure what to do."

"Call Tessa." Nicole's voice sounded hoarse from nervousness.

"I don't want to call her over every little thing." Claire looked out at the people strolling by the big glass window of the shop. "When I saw her last, she reassured me about my skills. I have to pay attention and figure it out."

Nicole said, "Tessa told you not to push. You're feeling tense. Try and clear your mind. Close your eyes for a minute and breathe deeply."

A wave of fatigue came over Claire and she felt like she'd have to sit in the chair for the rest of the day. Slumping down so she could lean her head back, she let her eyelids shut and she concentrated on breathing slowly and deeply. Whenever a thought or an image slid into her consciousness, she gently pushed it aside. The tension in her muscles melted away as her body warmed from the sun's rays coming in through the window and she slowly opened her eyes.

Nicole leaned closer. "Did it work? Did anything come to you?"

Claire shook her head. "Nothing, but I feel better now." Turning her head to watch the people moving along the sidewalk outside, she saw a business-woman catch her heel in the bricks and begin to fall forward. In an instant, an older woman coming from the opposite direction reached out and grabbed the falling woman's arm and kept her from hitting the ground. Claire watched as the grateful business-woman grasped her helper's hand and thanked her.

"Did you see that?" Claire asked. "If that woman didn't help, the other woman would have taken a nasty fall."

A bright light popped in Claire's head blinding her for an instant. *Help. Help.* She stood up so fast the chair almost toppled. "Can you and Robby handle things here for the rest of the afternoon without me? I need to go somewhere."

"Where? Should I go with you?" Nicole's face looked pale.

"We both can't leave the store." Claire pulled off her apron. "I'm not sure of anything yet. I want to check something out."

"Can't it wait until we close for the afternoon?"

"I don't think so." After rushing to the back room to grab her purse, Claire hurried to the door.

Nicole was on her feet. "Call me. Let me know what's going on."

HER MIND RACING, Claire practically ran down the sidewalks of the North End. The afternoon heat was strong and in no time, beads of sweat were running down her back. Thoughts swirled in her head, but were as scrambled as the eggs Vanessa made that morning. The combination of the heat, a sense of vertigo, and her hammering heart made Claire slow and step into the shade for a minute. With her legs feeling weak and rubbery, she knew she'd pass out before reaching the subway station so she decided to hail a cab to take her the rest of the way.

Seated in the vehicle, the cool air helped her feel less dizzy and as she tried to slow her breathing, she watched the buildings and people flash by as the car sped along the busy streets of Boston. Although her thoughts and the images in her head pointed to one thing, she wasn't clear about the meaning. She only knew she had to listen to her intuition and go check it out. As the taxi approached the building where Claire wanted to stop, she couldn't keep her heart beat from racing, and despite the comfortable temperature in the cab, her hands became clammy and cold.

Claire paid the driver, got out, and opened the door of the establishment. She stepped inside, moving her eyes over the patrons searching around for the person she wanted to speak with. A sigh of relief escaped her throat when she spotted the man leaning against the far end of the bar regaling a group of young women with a story.

Moving to stand behind the group, Claire caught

the man's attention and he glanced over, looked away, and then recognizing the athletic blonde, quickly returned his gaze to her.

Making eye contact with him, Claire spoke over the shoulder of one of the members of Bob Cooney's audience. "I need to ask you a favor."

25

Claire and Cooney moved to the other end of the polished bar.

"I didn't expect to see you again. Where's your friend?" Cooney eyed Claire with interest. "You need a job done or something?"

"Not exactly." Now that Claire was in the bar, she was unsure how to approach the subject she wanted to discuss with the private investigator.

"What is it then?" Cooney gulped a swallow of beer from the glass he'd carried with him and looked at Claire. "You want a drink or something?"

Shaking her head, Claire said, "I'm not sure how to ask my question."

Cooney grinned. "Just open your mouth and say

the words. What's the matter? You want me to kill someone for you?" When he saw the expression on Claire's face, he added quickly, "Only kidding, for Pete's sake. I draw the line at that." He smiled again. "But anything else is fair game."

"When my friend and I were here yesterday, we weren't exactly up front with you."

Cooney shrugged. "Wouldn't be the first time that's happened."

"We talked about Dr. Dodd," Claire said to jog the man's memory.

"Yeah, so?"

"Dr. Dodd is our friend's father."

"Go on."

"We should have said so, but...."

"No hard feelings." Cooney moved his hand in the air. "Get to the point."

"Dr. Dodd's been acting very odd."

"Surprise."

"No one knows if he killed his wife or Victoria Lowe, but something is wrong with him."

"You have strong reasoning skills," Cooney sassed Claire.

"You told us that Dr. Dodd said someone was after him."

Cooney cocked his head and leaned back against the bar.

Claire went on. "You told us the doctor had an apartment in the city."

"And?"

"Do you know where it is?"

"Yeah, I met him there a couple of times."

"Can you take me there?"

Cooney's eyes widened. "Why? The daughter want to shoot him or something?"

"It's just me. I'm alone."

"Why do you want to go that old goat's apartment?"

"Because I think he needs help."

Letting out a loud guffaw, Cooney said, "That's without a doubt."

"I'm serious," Claire told the man. "I think something's happened to him."

Narrowing his eyes, Cooney asked, "Why do you think that?"

"I don't have time to explain the whole thing. I need to get to him before it's too late."

"When you came in here, you said you had a favor to ask me." Cooney crossed his arms over his chest. "I don't do favors."

"Then will you do it as a job for me?"

"How much?" Cooney asked.

"How much would something like this cost me?"

"You want me to take you to the doc's apartment? Anything else?"

"Maybe break in to see if he's okay."

"That it?"

"If he's hurt, would you call it in for me?"

"No way. Absolutely not."

"Then let's hope he isn't hurt. My bank is two blocks from here. How much?"

Cooney said evenly, "Five thousand dollars."

Claire's jaw dropped. "You're kidding."

"I don't come cheap." Cooney sniffed.

Claire turned on her heel. "Let's go then."

WITH THE WAD of cash stuffed into his wallet, Bob Cooney sat in the cab with Claire on the way to the address he'd given.

"Near the Common," Claire noted.

"It's close to the hospital. The doc can claim he needs the place to crash after work when he's too tired or it's too late to go home." Cooney chuckled.

"The old goat doesn't use it when he's tired, no sir-ee."

Claire gave him a dirty look.

"Oh lighten up. Jeez." Cooney looked out the window. "Why is this so important to you?"

"Because it is." Claire's head was spinning again and she didn't care to engage in any conversation.

The cab came to a stop in front of a brick row house located in a well-heeled neighborhood and the two got out. "The doc has expensive taste. Better to impress the ladies." When he saw Claire's expression, he shrugged and got down to business. "You go up, knock on the door. If you need some ... ah, assistance getting the door open, come back down and get me. If you don't come down in ten minutes, I'm outta here."

"What if Dr. Dodd tries to hurt me?" Claire stared up at the building.

"You didn't hire me to be your bodyguard."

"That's extra, I suppose."

"Of course it is. It wouldn't be fair if you asked for one thing, I give you a price and then you start adding stuff on for free. I wouldn't be in business for long, would I?"

"Come up with me." Claire's resolve was fading. "Stand to the side. If the doctor comes to the door, then you can slip away. If he doesn't, then you can use your skills to get the door open and leave. It will save time if you come up with me now."

Cooney shrugged and followed Claire into the building. He pressed a code on the door to unlock it.

Claire glared at the man. "You didn't tell me there was a code. How was I supposed to get in?"

"I was planning to let you in, but I'm not telling you what the numbers are. That's private information given to me by the doctor." He held the door open for Claire and they went to the elevator, entered, and Cooney pushed the button for the fourth floor. They walked down the hallway together and Cooney gestured for Claire to knock.

"Don't tell Dodd it was me who told you where he lives," Cooney whispered and shuffled away so the doctor wouldn't see him when he opened the door. "If you need to get outta here in a hurry, the back staircase is that way." He pointed.

Taking in a deep breath, Claire raised her hand to knock, but she hesitated with her fist in the air. Pressing her fingers against the door, she closed her eyes trying to sense if the man was inside. A humming vibration buzzed in her fingertips and Claire pressed her whole hand against the door in an attempt to better feel the sensation.

An odd, metallic odor entered her nostrils and caught in her throat. Under her hand, the door felt as if it was moving in its frame and Claire opened her eyes to see.

The door was still. What was going on in there? A rush of anxiety flooded Claire's body and filled her with the urgent impulse to run. She wheeled around towards the elevator.

Cooney stood in the middle of the hall. He gestured a knocking movement. "Go on, knock," he said softly.

Claire steeled herself, turned back, and hit the door with her knuckles. It remained quiet inside so she rapped a few more times. When no one answered, she waved Cooney over. "Open it for me."

The man reached into his back pocket and removed a surgical glove and a slender, metal pick.

"Always prepared?" Claire asked.

Cooney wiggled the pick in the lock for a few seconds before it clicked. Turning the knob with the gloved hand, he opened the door a crack. "Do I get a bonus?"

"It was included in the money I already gave you." Her heart in her throat, Claire pushed the door open with her elbow not wanting to leave finger-prints. "Stay for a minute."

As they stepped into the shadowy room, the odor got stronger. The heavy drapes had been pulled closed making the place dark, but Claire could make out the high-end furnishings and expensive artwork on the walls. The doctor clearly liked nice things.

Moving slowly around the furniture grouping, Claire stopped short and gasped.

Cooney was on her heels. "What the...?" He let out a curse.

Dr. Dodd lay crumpled on the floor in front of the white sofa. Blood soaked the front of his shirt. Claire rushed to the man and felt his wrist for a pulse. "He's alive," she whispered.

"I'm outta here, lady. I'm not getting mixed up in this one. Keep my name out of it. Thanks for the cash." Cooney took off out of the place like a rocket.

Flicking her eyes frantically around the room for a landline phone, Claire spotted one on the desk near the window. Hurrying over, she pulled the bottom of her shirt from her slacks and used the hem to lift the phone from its cradle. She pressed the numbers, 911, with a pencil from the desk. After reporting the accident and the address, Claire carefully placed the receiver back on its cradle when the dispatcher asked for her name.

Taking the pencil with her, she scrambled for the

door, and pausing, she looked back at the uncon- scious body prone on the floor. "I can't stay here. There'd be no way to explain why I was in your apartment. Hang on. They're coming. Help's on the way."

26

Claire raced down the building's back staircase and slowed to a walk as soon as she was outside. Crossing the street to a small park, she shakily sat down on a bench and waited for the emergency personnel to arrive at Dodd's apartment. In a few minutes, she heard the siren approaching. *Thank heavens.* An ambulance pulled to the corner and a man and woman ran into the building.

After checking her clothes for any blood, Claire started walking back to Nicole's shop and the entire way her mind raced and her body flooded with guilt that she couldn't have stayed with the doctor until help arrived. Tears gathered in her eyes, but she pushed them away and wouldn't let them fall.

Although she wanted to alert Vanessa that her father had been injured and taken to the hospital, Claire had no idea how to explain her presence at the apartment. *I had a feeling. I sensed your father was in peril when I touched the watch that used to belong to him.* What nonsense. They'd send Claire for a psychological evaluation.

Claire's thoughts turned to a different concern. *Who attacked the doctor? How did the person know where the doctor's apartment was located?* Claire wanted to call Ian, but the same worries stopped her ... how could she explain what she knew and why she'd gone to find the doctor?

Nicole was just locking the front door of the shop when she spotted Claire coming towards her. "You look like a ghost. What on earth happened?"

Unable to hold it together any longer, tears cascaded down Claire's cheeks causing Nicole to grab her arm and steer her to the door of the building that led to Nicole's upstairs apartment. By the time they sat down, Claire had pulled herself together and she poured out the story of the past three hours.

"You can't feel guilty," Nicole declared. "You probably saved the doctor's life. You could not stay in the apartment with him for all of the reasons you just mentioned. I should have gone with you. What if the person who attacked Dr. Dodd was still in there?"

"Then I guess he would have attacked me, too," Claire mumbled weakly.

Nicole groaned. "You know ... my life was a lot less dramatic before I met you."

A little smile spread over Claire's lips. "You mean your life was a lot more *boring* before you met me."

"That, too." Nicole headed for her kitchen. "I'm going to make you some toast and tea. That will make you feel better." In a few minutes she returned to the sitting room with a tray carrying teacups, honey, and two small plates with buttered toast. "I decided it looked good so I'm having some, too."

Claire thanked her friend and slid a bit on the sofa cushion to get closer to the coffee table. "What should I do about telling Vanessa?"

"Nothing." Nicole added a spoonful of honey to her tea. "People know Dr. Dodd at the hospital. God, his face has been plastered all over the news, everyone must know who he is. Someone will notify her that he's been brought in."

"It feels awful to know and not tell her."

"It's the right thing to do. It will be okay." Nicole

tilted her head slightly. "What made you leave the chocolate shop so quickly to go to find Dr. Dodd?"

"When we were sitting by the window, remember we saw that woman trip and the other person help her? The word *help* kept echoing in my head. The other day, Tony told me that Dr. Dodd needed help and asked why no one was helping the man. He meant because Dodd seemed to be losing it, but when he said those words, they kept repeating in my head. When we were at the shop, it suddenly hit me that I needed to find Dr. Dodd. I knew he needed help." Claire shrugged.

"Well, I bet you saved his life." Nicole frowned. "Not sure that's a good thing."

"I know, but I had to do it."

"I understand. I would've done the same thing."

"I'm feeling on edge, Nic ... about the attacker. We need to figure out who did it."

"How can we do that?" Nicole didn't think it would be possible to determine who attacked Dodd. They had no clues and no one stood out. "He may have killed the two women who might've wanted revenge on him. Who's left who would want him dead? Could the attack have been random?"

"No," Claire's voice was emphatic. "It definitely wasn't random."

Nicole sucked in a nervous breath. "Not Vanessa or Maddy? It can't be them."

"I thought we took them off the suspect list when you and Vanessa found the rope in their kitchen? I was with Maddy and you were with Vanessa. Neither one had time alone to get the rope and drop it in the kitchen." Claire shook her head. "No, I don't feel that either one has anything to do with any part of this mess."

Nicole slumped back against the cushion. "Except live in the mess that somebody made for them."

Claire looked across the room, focusing on nothing. Her chest tightened, a rope of anxiety choking her. "Something's on the air."

Nicole shifted her eyes to her friend and waited.

"We need to figure it out. Fast." The muscles in Claire's body tensed and she whispered, "I feel like it's right in front of us, staring us in the face."

"Don't get all wonky on me." Nicole could feel the anxiety and sense of panic pouring off of Claire. "You just came back from a horrible scene. You cannot start getting all shook up again. It's important to stay level-headed. Listen, Dr. Dodd will wake up and he'll be able to tell the police about his attacker."

"You're right." Claire tried the breathing-deeply method to calm herself. "I need to clear my head."

"Maybe the doctor even knows the person who attacked him," Nicole offered cheerfully. "Then the guy will be in custody before we know it."

Claire sat bolt upright. "I think he *does* know the person who attacked him. But how would he? Who could it be?"

Nicole sat straight. "What about Bob Cooney? He doesn't exactly seem like an upstanding guy. He might have killed Dodd over money. He could have easily gone back to the bar after he killed him so he'd have an alibi."

"I don't think it's Cooney." Ice cold anxiety gripped Claire's stomach. "And I don't think the doctor is going to wake up in time to stop what's going to happen next."

Nicole shivered. "You're scaring me."

Claire stood up and started pacing around the room. "Think. We have to think." She walked up and down the length of the living room for a few minutes before wheeling around. "Cooney told us Dr. Dodd was paranoid. The doctor thought someone was after him." Ideas swirled in her head. "If that's true, who would it be? Who might be angry at him besides his daughters?"

"Well, he's a doctor. One of his patients could be angry over something." Nicole had another idea. "Or one of the women he dated and ditched might want to get back at him."

Pieces of the puzzle began to align in Claire's mind. "You're a genius. I bet that could be it, one of his patients." She said excitedly, "Let's look up Dr. Dodd. Look for any malpractice cases against him."

They moved to the kitchen table and after a few clicks on the keyboard, pages of information showed on the screen.

"Here are some things." Nicole leaned forward to better read the information.

It took more than fifteen minutes to sort through the material on the computer and to follow from one thread to another. They were about to give up on the idea when Nicole said, "Wait a minute." She pointed to the words on the laptop with a shaky finger. "Look at this."

Claire read what it said. "Geoffrey Matthew McAdams vs. Dr. Ronald Dodd." Her vision began to spin. "Matthew McAdams ... Matthew Adams, that's the name of the guy Vanessa was dating. He's using only part of his name. What does the article say?"

Nicole paraphrased. "McAdams's wife died while in surgery with Dr. Dodd. It was a second surgery.

The first one didn't go well so Dodd did a different procedure, but was unable to save the woman. McAdams sued. The doctor was cleared of any wrong-doing."

"Is there a picture of this McAdams person?" Claire asked.

Nicole tapped at the keys and let out a gasp. "It's him. The guy we met." She looked up at Claire. "Oh, no. It's Vanessa's Matthew, isn't it? This is too weird. He sued the doctor over his wife's death and didn't get satisfaction from the court or medical board." Nicole's hand went to her throat. "Did he take things into his own hands and try to kill the doctor?"

"Every time Vanessa brought that guy up, I got a strange feeling. Maddy didn't like him when she met him. He's started harassing Vanessa recently."

"So what? He attacks Dr. Dodd because he lost the case against him?" Nicole narrowed her eyes. "He starts dating the doctor's daughter? Why?"

"To get back at the doctor," Claire suggested.

Nicole shook her head. "It can't be true. It's too outlandish."

Claire leveled her eyes at her friend. "Isn't everything about this case outlandish?"

"Are we jumping to conclusions? Is this possible?"

"His wife died under the doctor's care. He sued, but didn't get the outcome he hoped for. Vanessa said that Matthew isn't someone who appreciates the word *no*. If he was angry enough ... who knows?"

Nicole's phone buzzed with a text. "It's Vanessa. She's at the hospital. Her father has been stabbed and is in critical condition, but is expected to live. He's unconscious. She's going to stay there."

Nicole sent off a text with words of sympathy and a question asking if the police knew who attacked her father. She read the reply aloud. "No one knows who did it."

Claire's heart thudded. "Ask Vanessa if Maddy is with her."

Nicole sent the text and an answer came in almost immediately. "It says, 'Maddy wouldn't come with me to the hospital. She stayed at Claire's.'"

Claire stood up, her blue eyes dark. "Maddy." The word was like a wisp on the air.

An expression of alarm washed over Nicole's face. "Oh, no."

27

"Call Maddy," Claire grabbed her bag. "Tell her to keep the door locked and if anyone knocks or rings, don't answer the door."

"Do you think Matthew is going to try and hurt Maddy and Vanessa?" Nicole wanted desperately to hear Claire say no, but she knew what the answer would be.

"I think they should be cautious until the police can check Matthew out."

"She isn't answering." Nicole's voice held a tone of panic.

"Leave a message. Tell her to call you back as soon as she hears it." Claire called a cab and it met them outside Nicole's apartment.

"At least the dogs are with her," Nicole said as she settled into the back seat of the taxi.

"I left the dogs with Tony." Claire's face was tense.

Nicole quickly placed another call to Maddy. "Why won't she answer?"

As soon as she clicked off, the phone tweeted.

"It's Maddy," Nicole said with relief and talked into the phone. "Claire and I are on our way back to her place. We'll see you in a few minutes."

Nicole listened to Maddy's reply and then she turned to Claire. "Maddy isn't at your townhouse. She went home to get some things."

Claire groaned and gave the address in Greendale to the cab driver while Nicole gave Maddy instructions about locking up and not answering if someone came to the door.

"Be ready to leave when we get there. I'm sure everything will be fine, but precautions need to be taken because of the attack on your father," Nicole told the girl. "Wait for us. We'll pick you up and then head back to Claire's house."

Nicole ended the call and let out a sigh of relief. "I feel better now that I've talked to her."

"I don't." Claire watched out the window at the city shrouded in darkness. Clenching and unclenching her fists, she counted the seconds until they arrived at the Dodds's house.

"Will you wait?" Claire asked the driver after he pulled to the curb. "We won't be long."

Claire and Nicole got out of the cab and moved up the walkway to the grand front porch. Lights shined in several of the downstairs windows. Claire rang the bell.

Nicole nervously looked back to be sure the cab was still at the curb.

When no one answered, the young women exchanged quick glances and as waves of unease pounded at Claire, she pressed the bell a second time.

As soon as Maddy clicked off from Nicole, she hurried to her room to find some books from last semester's classes that she wanted to go over again before the fall term started. She shoved them into the duffel bag along with some clothes and toiletries and then swung the bag over her shoulder to head back downstairs. Pausing at the threshold, she let her eyes rove over her room, the bed, the bookshelves, her desk, the curtains her mother had helped her pick out. A heavy sense of loss nearly crushed her, and despite the rage she harbored for her father, she thought about him resting on a hospital bed fighting for his life and her heart contracted. Part of her never wanted to see the man again, yet another part wanted to rush to his side and hold his hand. *How did this happen to our family? How did things go so wrong?*

The doorbell rang and Maddy left her room with a confused and heavy heart. She dropped her bag in the foyer and went to open the door, surprised that Nicole and Claire had arrived so fast.

"I'm almost ready," Maddy said as she unlocked the door and swung it open. When she saw who was standing there under the porch light, panic shot through her body.

"Hi, Maddy." The man smiled, but his eyes were dark and intense. His form took up most of the doorway.

The young woman's senses screamed a warning and she took a step back and pushed the door as hard as she could.

Matthew McAdams lunged, stopped the door from slamming in his face, grabbed Maddy by the arm and shoved her into the foyer, and with one smooth movement, kicked the door shut with his foot.

"Why don't you call her and tell her we're here." Claire shifted nervously from foot to foot. "She might be afraid to answer the door."

Nicole made the call, but all it did was ring and ring and ring. "Nothing."

Claire stepped off the porch, tilted her head, and looked up to the dark, second floor rooms.

"What should we do?" Nicole asked. "Go around back?"

"Let's go take a look. Maybe she's in the kitchen." Claire started to walk around to the rear of the house.

"Maybe the bell is broken," Nicole said hopefully as she started down the steps.

"But, I heard it ring." Claire stopped and looked back at the front door and unease wrapped itself around her throat. She moved up the steps past Nicole, walked to the door, took the handle in her hand, and turned it. It clicked open.

A waterfall of anxiety crashed over Claire's head,

and giving Nicole a look of alarm, she lifted her index finger to her lips, and whispered, "Shh."

FROM THE FOYER, Matthew pulled Maddy by her long hair into Dr. Dodd's office and shoved her across the room.

"What do you want?" Maddy glared at Matthew and despite the fear racing through her body, she made the decision that if she had to, she would fight this man to the death.

"I want to hurt your father." Sweat beaded up on Matthew's forehead.

"It was you, wasn't it?" Maddy growled. "You attacked my father, didn't you?"

"Why didn't you go the hospital with your sister?"

"None of your business."

"I think you didn't go because you hate your father." Matthew sneered at Maddy trying to unnerve her.

"Think what you want." Maddy moved her feet backwards to position herself behind the desk. A pile of items had been placed on the desktop when Vanessa and Maddy removed the things from the floor after their father's office had been trashed by the intruder. Papers, pencils, binders, and folders were scattered over the smooth dark wood ... and something else was there that interested Maddy ... a pair of scissors.

The man laughed. "Big talk for a little girl."

"What do you have against my father?" Maddy wanted to keep the man talking.

Matthew's facial expression turned hard and cold and his eyes had a crazy look to them. "He killed my wife."

"Was she a patient?"

Matthew ignored the question. "He killed my wife ... so I killed his."

Maddy's throat constricted. "You ... killed my mother?"

"And now I'm going to kill the rest of the family."

Maddy's head spun and her vision began to dim, but she shook herself and forced her voice to be strong and even. "He isn't dead, you know. My father is going to live."

"Good," Matthew jeered. "Then he'll be alive to mourn the death of his daughters." His started his advance on Maddy, moving slowly and menacingly towards the desk.

Maddy waited. She knew she'd have to be quick.

As the man lunged to wrap his hands around Maddy's neck, her fingers scrambled over the desk to grab the scissors.

His big hands tightened on her throat.

Maddy lifted her arm and slashed at Matthew's face just as Claire and Nicole rushed through the door.

Claire jumped onto the man's back, wrapped her arm around his throat, and pummeled him with her fist. Matthew lost his balance and he and Claire crashed to the floor.

Nicole grabbed a pedestal lamp and smashed it over the fallen man's head as Claire rolled to the side.

Matthew screamed and covered his head with his arms as Ian Fuller dashed into the room with his gun drawn.

Nicole hurried behind the desk and took Maddy into her arms.

"I'm okay," Maddy said, her body shaking. "I'm okay."

Claire pushed herself up off the floor, walked to Maddy and Nicole and put her arms around them. She smiled with relief at Ian who had his phone to his ear and his gun pointed at Matthew.

Ian turned his eyes to Claire and his smile warmed her heart.

"I texted Ian from the cab while you were talking to Maddy," Claire told Nicole. "I thought we might need some backup."

"Smart," Nicole said, still holding tight to the young woman in her arms. "But we did pretty well on our own, didn't we?"

Claire hugged them as tightly as she could.

28

Under a bright blue sky, Claire, Nicole, and Augustus sat at the patio table on the sidewalk outside of Tony's market. Fruits and vegetables were displayed on a covered wooden cart to the side of the front entrance to his store and blue ceramic pots spilled over with summer flowers. The Corgis sat in the shade of the building next to the table watching the people passing by.

Ian Fuller and his friend, Detective Miles who served the Greendale area, sat opposite Augustus and the two women.

Tony carried out a tray of iced tea and placed a glass in front of everyone. He pulled up a metal chair and squeezed in to listen to the updates on the Dodd case.

Detective Miles said, "Geoffrey Matthew McAdams, also known as Matthew Adams, is in custody and has confessed to the attack on Dr. Dodd and the murder of Grace Dodd. McAdams harbors rage against the doctor for the death of his own wife so he came up with a plot to get back at him by killing his family. McAdams broke into the house the night Vanessa and Maddy went to the Opera House. He found Dr. Dodd asleep in his room. Mrs. Dodd ran into McAdams in the hall, they fought, she broke away, ran to the third floor, and was pushed from the window to her death."

The detective went on. "Dr. Dodd heard some noise, but was drowsy because he'd taken a sleeping pill earlier in the evening. He managed to rouse himself, but by then it was too late. McAdams had already run from the house to the backyard. He stood at the tree line waiting to see if the doctor would get up to investigate." Detective Miles shook his head. "He wanted to see the man's reaction."

Claire and Nicole exchanged disgusted glances.

"That's who Maddy saw standing near the trees that night," Claire said.

Detective Miles said, "After killing Mrs. Dodd,

McAdams was to leave for Cape Cod. He had made plans to meet Vanessa there to spend the day on his boat."

"Didn't he think that Vanessa would cancel after she discovered her mother had died?" Claire asked.

"He made those plans to give himself an alibi." The detective shifted in his seat. "McAdams had other plans, as well ... after some time had passed, he was going to suggest to Vanessa that she meet him at his boat for a day cruise as a break from her troubles. Once at sea, he would push her over and leave her there to drown."

Nicole let out a gasp.

Ian said, "McAdams was the one who broke into the Dodds's house and ransacked the doctor's office."

"Why did he do it?" Claire questioned.

"He thought Dodd might have some incriminating evidence in his office about his handling of McAdams's wife's surgeries," Detective Miles said.

"He was planning to attack Vanessa and Maddy the night you were both there with the dogs," Ian told them. "He heard the dogs, realized there were more people in the house than he could handle so took off."

Nicole's fingers rubbed at her temple and her

voice shook. "He was going to kill Vanessa and Maddy that night."

Augustus spoke up. "Will Dr. Dodd have a full recovery?"

"He is expected to." Detective Miles nodded. "He's fully conscious and doing well. We've had several chats with the man."

Augustus asked, "Why was Dr. Dodd's behavior so strange during this time? Was the shock of his wife's death too much for the man?"

Miles set down his glass of iced tea. "Dr. Dodd felt responsible for his wife's death. He suffered heavy guilt believing that their fights over his infidelity turned Grace to suicide. He was sure she jumped from the window."

Nicole said, "Vanessa and Maddy never believed Grace died from suicide. They were right."

"Who discovered Dr. Dodd in his apartment after he was attacked by McAdams?" Tony asked.

"That is unknown," Miles replied. "The woman didn't give her name. Most likely someone living in the building. Maybe the door to the apartment was ajar and the woman went in to see if anything was wrong. Whoever it was, she saved the doctor's life."

Augustus turned his head and gave Claire a look.

Claire knew that Augustus had guessed that she

was the one who found Dodd in the apartment. She shifted her gaze away and brought up something else. "And what about Dr. Dodd's lover, Representative Lowe? Did McAdams kill her, too, as part of his revenge on the doctor?"

"He did not," Miles said. "He claims to have had nothing to do with the woman's death."

Ian told the group, "Dr. Dodd has given his version of what happened that day in Victoria Lowe's townhouse." He looked at Miles and, with a hand gesture, the detective encouraged Ian to report the details.

"Dr. Dodd was distraught about his wife's accident believing she took her own life. Despite being in love with Ms. Lowe, he went to her townhouse to break off their affair. He revealed part of their conversation to us, stating that when he told his lover he wanted to end things, she was in a state of disbelief thinking that the stress of Grace's death and the distrust of Dodd's daughters towards the man had pushed the doctor into a state of shock. She talked to him about it, but Dr. Dodd said he was so distraught that he had to end their relationship. Ms. Lowe became furious. Her own marriage was about to end. Her husband had recently discovered the affair and had filed for divorce. Dr. Dodd said Ms.

Lowe was ranting at him as she headed for the basement to get her laundry. She told him to collect himself and think about what he was doing and when she came up from the basement that he better be more reasonable. As she was yelling at Dodd, she missed the top of the step and fell down the staircase landing hard on the concrete floor."

Claire realized that what she felt in her chest when she was in the alley behind Ms. Lowe's townhouse was the woman's heart being broken by Dr. Dodd.

Miles took up the story. "Dodd told us he ran to the woman, checked her pulse, and immediately knew she was dead. He panicked and ran from the home afraid if he called the police, they'd arrest him. He said no one would ever believe that Ms. Lowe's death had been an accident."

Ian added, "Not after Grace Dodd's accident. Two women tied to Dr. Dodd died within days of each other. The doctor was right. It would have been very difficult for the police to believe the two events were accidents."

Miles said, "The doctor's mental decline accelerated after Ms. Lowe's death. He also believed that McAdams was after him and he was terrified."

"Why didn't Dodd link McAdams to his wife's

fall from the window?" Claire's voice held an angry tone.

"He was sure that Grace had jumped." Miles shook his head. "The doctor's reasoning had become seriously impaired."

Nicole frowned. "By keeping silent about his fear that McAdams was after him, he put his wife and daughters at risk."

"Vanessa said she met McAdams at a coffee shop," Claire said. "He must have found out Dodd had daughters and then stalked her?"

"Basically, that was it," Miles said. "He followed Vanessa around for weeks. One day, he approached her in a crowded coffee shop and asked if he could sit at her table. He chatted with her and asked her to have a drink later that night."

"Vanessa always seemed hesitant about Matthew. She must have sensed his dishonesty."

"How's Maddy doing after being attacked by that devil?" Tony huffed.

Nicole smiled. "Amazingly well. She seems confidant and self-assured, almost like she feels gratified that she had a hand in taking down her mother's killer."

"She sure was brave," Claire added. "That girl is a fighter."

"And how about Vanessa?" Tony asked.

"She's strong, too," Nicole said. "She is struggling with falling for Matthew's deception, but I reminded her that she knew something was off with the guy. She listened to her intuition."

Miles said, "Dr. Dodd had everything … money, a nice family, prestige, professional respect. Then he turned his life and many other people's lives to ruin. Quite a reversal of fortune."

Claire looked up to see Robby hurry around the corner.

"Here you all are," he said with a broad smile. "I texted Nicole and she told me she was at Tony's."

"You look awfully happy." Nicole eyed the young man.

"Did you win the lottery or something?" Tony chuckled.

"Practically." Robby pulled a chair up to the already crowded table. He was about to answer Tony when a sheepish look came over him. "Oh, sorry. Am I interrupting? I'm so excited I just barged right in."

"It's okay," Nicole put her hand on Robby's shoulder. "Do you have some good news?"

A wide grin spread over his face. "Guess what? You'll never believe it." Robby paused for a split second and then the words spilled in a torrent.

"The financial aid office called. They found a benefactor for me." His head spun from person to person. "The benefactor is paying off all of my loans and will be paying for my final year of schooling."

A cheer went up from the people around the table and the Corgis danced around Robby's chair.

Ian laughed. "I'm guessing you didn't have any money to pay for your last year of college?"

"Until now." Robby grinned from ear to ear.

"Well," Ian said. "Here's a different reversal of fortune. This one from bad to good."

"Do you know the person's name who's gifting you all this money?" Tony asked.

"Anonymous," Robby told them.

Again, Augustus gave Claire a sly look, but she pretended not to see his face.

"How come every time we sit out here in the sun," Tony asked with a happy smile, "someone gets a windfall?" Tony was referring to the day when a courier arrived to tell him that an anonymous donor had purchased for him the building that housed his market and his apartment.

"Maybe we should sit together out here more often," Ian suggested. "Maybe it will be *me* next time who gets a load of money handed to him."

Everyone laughed and stood for a minute to hug or shake hands with Robby.

"I guess someone didn't want all that talent going to waste." Claire rubbed Robby's shoulder.

"I'm so happy I could stand up and sing," Robby told the group.

"Do it," Claire said.

"Nope." Robby smirked and eyed Ian. "I don't want to get arrested for disturbing the peace."

Tony stood up to go inside the market. "This calls for a celebration. I'm going to go get a big cake and some paper plates."

A woman in a long colorful dress walked towards the group and Claire smiled and raised her hand to wave. "You'd better bring one more plate," she told Tony.

Tony looked up to see Tessa coming up beside him and the big man's face brightened.

Tessa's auburn hair glistened in the sunshine. "Are you having a party?"

"Join us." Claire told the woman about Robby's good news.

"Do you mind?" Tessa's eyes sparkled when she looked at Tony.

"It would be a pleasure." Tony beamed at her.

Claire wasn't sure what her answer would be if

someone asked who looked happier, Robby or Tony, but it didn't matter because the joy coming off of them danced on the air and filled Claire's heart to bursting. Cocking her head towards Tessa and Tony, she leaned towards Augustus with a wicked smile. "Later today?"

"Oh, my, yes." Augustus winked. "Tony is in for some wicked teasing."

As the sun pushed up over the horizon, Claire let out a yawn while helping Ian load the bikes on the bike rack attached to the back of his car.

Ian chuckled. "Will you be able to stay awake long enough to finish the race?"

"I think I could have used another week to train."

"You're ready," Ian encouraged. "You're going to do fine."

"I'm nervous." Claire wiped her sweaty hands on her shorts.

"Just pretend everyone around you is me. Then you'll sprint past all of them like you do when you trick me and bolt away when we're running down Beacon Street."

Raising an eyebrow, Claire said, "Maybe that will be my strategy. Act weak, and then strike."

"It works on me." Ian pulled the strap to tighten the bikes into place as Claire reached up to adjust one of the bicycle wheels and their arms brushed against one another.

The touch of Ian's skin on hers sent a jolt of electricity through Claire's veins and she had to lean down to pretend to fiddle with something in her gym bag so Ian wouldn't see her fluster.

"Shall we?" Ian gestured to the car.

Claire gave a nod and lifted her bag. "Nicole, Robby, Vanessa, and Maddy are going to meet us there."

"We'll have our own personal cheering section." Ian tossed his bag into the back seat and got in on the driver's side.

Claire settled next to him on the passenger seat.

"Thanks for letting me train with you." Ian started the engine. "I really wouldn't have been able to keep motivated without you."

Claire smiled at the handsome detective. "You did the same for me."

"We should keep training together. We can find another event to do." Ian pulled the car away from the curb.

"That would be great. As long as it's not a marathon."

"I was thinking...." Ian seemed hesitant, but then he finished the sentence. "There's this really nice restaurant not far from the triathlon course. I've read about it, but I've never been there."

Claire's heart jumped.

"I was wondering, if you don't need to get back right away, maybe we could have dinner there together before heading home."

Claire was so busy swooning, she could barely get the words out of her throat. "I'd love that."

Ian looked over at the pretty blond sitting just a foot away from him. "So would I," he told her. "So would I."

———————

I HOPE you enjoyed *Reversal of Fortune*! The next book in the series, *Murder and Misfortune*, can be found here:

getbook.at/MurderMisfortune

THANK YOU FOR READING!

Books by J.A. WHITING can be found here:
www.amazon.com/author/jawhiting

To hear about new books and book sales, please sign
up for my mailing list at:
www.jawhiting.com

Your email will never be sold, shared, or spammed.

If you enjoyed the book, please consider leaving a
review. A few words are all that's needed. It would be
very much appreciated.

ALSO BY J.A. WHITING

OLIVIA MILLER MYSTERIES (not cozy)

SWEET COVE COZY MYSTERIES

LIN COFFIN COZY MYSTERIES

CLAIRE ROLLINS COZY MYSTERIES

PAXTON PARK COZY MYSTERIES

SEEING COLORS MYSTERIES

ELLA DANIELS COZY WITCH MYSTERIES

SWEET BEGINNINGS BOX SETS

SWEET ROMANCES by JENA WINTER

ABOUT THE AUTHOR

J.A. Whiting lives with her family in Massachusetts. Whiting loves reading and writing mystery and suspense stories.

Visit / follow me at:
   www.jawhiting.com
   www.bookbub.com/authors/j-a-whiting
   www.amazon.com/author/jawhiting
   www.facebook.com/jawhitingauthor

Made in the USA
Monee, IL
28 January 2022

90066590R10173